*Four Historical Romances from
the Legendary American West*

Old West
Summer
BRIDES

The 12 Brides of Summer: *Book 3*

MARY CONNEALY, SUSAN PAGE DAVIS,
MIRALEE FERRELL, DAVALYNN SPENCER

BARBOUR BOOKS
An Imprint of Barbour Publishing, Inc.

Published by Barbour Books, an imprint of Barbour Publishing, Inc., P.O. Box 719, Uhrichsville, Ohio 44683, www.barbourbooks.com

Our mission is to publish and distribute inspirational products offering exceptional value and biblical encouragement to the masses.

Member of the
Evangelical Christian
Publishers Association

Printed in the United States of America.

A BRIDE
RIDES HERD

Mary Connealy

Chapter 1

Montanta
July 23, 1894

Matt heard the scream and whirled in his saddle.

A fast-moving creek barreled down the mountainside, and the scream came from that direction. Another scream, louder, higher up, from someone else.

Matt vaulted from his gelding and sprinted toward that water.

He cleared the heavy stand of ponderosa pines in time to hear another scream and see someone drowning, swept along by the current at breathtaking speed.

The creek was narrow, but it plunged down a mountainside. So did whoever was drowning.

Matt saw a spot just ahead littered with stones. Branches snarled up, damming the creek and making it deeper

7

without slowing it down.

Whoever had fallen in would be smashed to bits on this barrier, and if they somehow got swept past it, there was a waterfall a few dozen yards ahead.

He leaped up on the boulder closest to the bank and slipped. His boots weren't made for rock climbing.

There was no time to shed them.

"Grab my hand!"

The youngster, because Matt saw now it was a child careening down the rapids, turned to look at him then went under. Matt assumed this wasn't deep water, how could it be when it was rushing downhill, but it was deep enough for a child to submerge. He caught himself holding his own breath as if he'd gone under. He stepped across the stones, picking his way.

Ready.

He'd have one chance to grab this child, a girl, he saw long blond braids, and then he'd never see her again.

Heart pounding, Matt dropped to his knees and extended his arms to the limit. The child raced toward him. A tree just upstream of the rocks bent low enough. . . Matt was going to lose sight of the little one for a few crucial seconds right before he had to make his grab.

Then the child vanished behind the branches.

Matt braced himself to not let go and not get swept off the rocks.

The tree suddenly bowed until the branch looked ready

to snap. Then it whipped up and the child went flying into the air, kicked her legs hard, and swung to the shore, landing neatly.

Another scream. A second child.

Now Matt barely had time to gather his thoughts and get ready when the tree bowed again, snapped up, and another little girl went sailing upward, swung, and landed right where the first had.

Matt sprang to his feet as the two laughed hysterically.

One, slightly smaller than the other, said, "Let's go again!"

His knees almost buckled, and he jumped across the rocks to get out of the water. He didn't want to finish this off by falling in.

Then he really saw them.

White-blond hair, skinny, wild—Matt had a gut-wrenching suspicion. "Are you by any chance named Reeves?"

The two spun to look at him, ready to run, he thought. Good self-preservation instincts. To stop them he said, "I'm your Uncle Matt. Mark Reeves is my brother."

The older child edged back, but her eyes were full of fascination. "We've got lots of uncles. You aren't one of them."

Imagining them running upstream and casting themselves into the water again, Matt said, "I haven't ever been to visit before. Can you take me to your pa and ma?"

"Nope." The older one seemed to do the talking for both. Matt had heard about Mark's three daughters.

"You're Annie, right?" Matt said. That earned their full attention. He then turned to the littler girl. "And you're Susie."

Both girls' eyes went round with amazement. "You know our names?"

"Sure I do. Mark, your pa, writes home about you a lot." Well, about once per child and those letters came from his wife, Emma. "And I know you've got a little baby sister named Lilly. Let's go home."

He had to get them away from this wild stretch of water and tell Mark what he'd caught his children doing. Even as he trembled in fear he thought of all the crazy stunts he and his brothers, including Mark—especially Mark—had gotten up to over the years.

But that was different, they were boys.

Little girls were supposed to stay to the house and be quiet and sweet. Like his ma.

"We'll take you to our house, but we can't take you to Pa." Annie reached out and took his hand. She looked to be about six, though Matt knew nothing of girls and could only guess. Susie took Matt's other hand. The sweetest, softest hands he's ever felt. Matt realized right then that he loved his little nieces with his whole heart.

"I have to bring my horse." He tugged on their hands, and they came along happily. Susie even skipped a few steps. Matt couldn't stop himself from smiling.

They were beautiful little girls. He'd never met Mark's wife, Emma, but she must be a pretty thing.

They found Matt's horse, grazing where he'd ground hitched it, and Annie ran forward to grab the reins, then led the horse back to Matt and took his hand again.

They headed off in the direction Matt had planned to ride.

"What do you mean you can't take me to your pa?" It hit him that maybe something had happened. Matt had been roving for a long time. For all he knew his brother could be long dead and buried.

"He's on a cattle drive."

Matt's panic ended before it had fully begun. "So we'll go see your ma then."

"Nope." Annie gave him a look like he was stupid, but if her ma and pa were both gone then—

"Annie! Susie, where are you?" A voice that sounded like a woman being gnawed on by wolves cut through the clear mountain air.

"That's Aunt Betsy. She screams a lot." Annie shrugged one shoulder as if to say her aunt's ways were a complete mystery.

"It sounds like she's worried about you." As well she should be. "I'd better answer her," Matt said quietly then he shouted, "They're over here."

Pounding footsteps came at him through the dense

woods. Aunt Betsy sounded like she weighed three hundred pounds.

Then a beautiful woman with hair and eyes so dark she couldn't possibly be related to these girls, charged into view. Not three hundred pounds. Not. Even. Close. She had a white-haired baby on her slender hip, and the tyke was clinging for dear life.

She skidded to a stop when she saw Matt, and, faster than a man could blink, she drew a gun, cocked it, and said in a dark, dangerous voice, "Get away from those children."

Matt raised his hands, stunned at the dead serious look in Aunt Betsy's sparking black eyes. Trouble was, the girls had a firm grip. When he raised his hands, they clung and he lifted them right off the ground. They started squealing, and the fire in Aunt Betsy's eyes seemed to take their glee for alarm.

Quick before she pulled the trigger, he said, "I'm Mark's brother, come to visit. I found the girls, and they were showing me the way home. You must be Aunt Betsy."

Betsy kept her gun level and cocked. "You have the look of your brother, I'll give you that."

Matt had the impression that Betsy was inclined to shoot first and sort things out later—which Matt conceded spoke well of her protective instincts. But that didn't mean he wanted to be full of bullet holes out of respect for her vigilance.

"He knew our names, Aunt Betsy," Annie-the-Talker said. "Even Lilly's."

Then Matt remembered the tone of pure panic in Aunt Betsy's voice and the speed at which she'd come running. He knew something that would distract her. "I found them riding the creek down the mountainside. Looks like they're old hands at it."

Those black eyes went so wide with fear, Matt could see white all the way around her dark pupils.

"Girls, I told you to stay out of that creek." Her eyes, formerly trained on him, now looked at the soaking wet girls. "Your ma and pa told you clear as day it was dangerous." Betsy lowered the gun, looking mighty defeated.

Matt suspected that if she was in charge of these two, and with a baby on her hip besides, well. . .after knowing his nieces for around ten minutes, he felt some sympathy for pretty Aunt Betsy.

"Let's go back to the house, girls." It looked like his life was out of jeopardy from poor Aunt Betsy, but he wanted to be farther from that rushing, rocky creek.

Betsy's lip quivered and she nodded, shoving her gun into a pocket in her skirt that looked like it'd been sewn for just that purpose, as the gun fit perfectly. She came toward him, her shoulders slumped.

Lilly, who looked too young to walk, bounced on Betsy's hip and giggled then reached out her arms to Matt and said, "Papa."

Matt had been holding babies since before he was even close to old enough. He saw the launch coming, and Betsy must be an old hand, too, because she didn't let Lilly hurl herself to the ground.

Matt took the baby without dropping his horse's reins, and earned a grin with four teeth. Nine months old at the most. "Howdy, Lilly. I'm your Uncle Matt." He tickled her under her chin.

Betsy took Susie's hand and tried to take Annie's. The older girl dodged and caught hold of Matt's arm. He quit tickling and let himself be guided through woods so dense no sunlight reached the ground. There was no trail Matt could see, but the girls seemed familiar with the woods, pretty surprising when this was an area forbidden to them.

Well, Ma had done her share of "forbidding" with Matt and his brothers. And she'd had poor luck earning their obedience—though he wasn't sure she ever realized it.

The woods thinned out and Matt saw the house and was surprised by his pang of envy.

Chapter 2

Betsy saw the house and was all too familiar with the pang of terror.

Emma was going to kill her if she came home and found both girls had died or run off or been kidnapped by roving outlaws. Oh, there were a hundred ways to come to grief in the West. And that was if you were careful. These girls didn't show one speck of caution. . .which meant there were a thousand ways to die.

"Nice house," Matt said, sounding almost reverent. Polite, too, and smart enough. His horse looked like it was well cared for. He wore a gun as if he knew how to use it.

Betsy decided then and there to do some kidnapping herself. Matt Reeves wasn't going anywhere until his brother came home.

"I'll have the noon meal ready in an hour, Matt. Turn your horse into the corral and come on in."

She wondered if she should pick her moment and hide his horse or depend on her feminine wiles to get him to stay.

Not that she had any feminine wiles. Ma hadn't been of much use when it came to teaching such things. Belle Harden was more the type to advise her daughters on how to run men off. Betsy was a hand at it, and she had Pa and Ma to help. . .even when she didn't want help.

And that's how she'd ended up a near spinster. Eighteen years old and not a beau to be found.

She was too busy most of the time to care, but a girl had a few daydreams.

"I'll be right in." Matt, the gullible fool, handed Lilly over. The baby screamed and cried and threw herself at Matt.

Well, Betsy had been handling babies from her first memory, so Lilly didn't manage to cast herself onto the ground, but it was a near thing.

Susie escaped while Betsy wrestled Lilly. Then Matt plucked the baby out of her arms, Susie took Annie's hand, and the four of them. . .five counting the horse, left Betsy behind.

She started to yell warnings to Matt but figured anything she warned him of would just give the girls inspiration.

She was abandoning those girls to a stranger, and she

dreaded it. Not because of danger to the girls. Nope. She was purely afraid Matt was going to come to his senses and run off.

Heading for the house to make the best meal she could manage, she wondered just what the man was made of. Those girls would soon reveal his every weakness.

Matt snatched Annie out from under the restless hooves of his horse just as Susie climbed to the top of the pen that held a snorting, pawing, mama longhorn.

Faster than he ever had in his life, Matt stripped the leather from his horse, with a baby in his arms, then went to turn his gelding loose in a stall that stank of dirty straw.

What was going on here? Who was tending this barn?

He shooed the horse out into the corral, while juggling all three girls. Doing the minimum while saving the girls' lives at every turn, he was an hour getting to the most basic chores.

More attention should be paid to the barn, and the stalls needed forking and his horse needed hay. Then he thought of pitching some of the lush hay filling the mow in Mark's barn down for his horse, and imagined taking all three girls up there. He ran for the house with them before he lost one permanently. Betsy could watch them while he did chores.

He shoved them inside, thinking to slam the door and

run. Then he smelled sizzling steaks.

His favorite.

"Dinner's ready." Betsy was just about the most beautiful girl Matt had ever seen. Not that he'd seen many girls. Not that many wandering in the mountains, and that's where Matt had been for the last few years.

But she was the prettiest, bar none. And while he was at it, staring at that thick curling black hair and those big shining eyes and her tempting pink lips, he decided she was the most beautiful woman ever, including all the ones he'd never seen.

There couldn't be one more beautiful.

Maybe her lips were tempting because she was talking about food and he was just plain starving. Especially starving for a meal cooked by a woman's hand.

He'd eaten a lot of roasted rabbit, quail, and trout. It was tasty, but some variety was tempting indeed.

He should go back out and clean out that stall and turn his horse into it and water and hay him, then hit the trail and give Mark a week or two to come home.

She pulled lightly browned biscuits out of a cast-iron oven and moved a halfway-to-done pie to the center.

Pie and biscuits.

Matt wasn't going anywhere. He was as surely caught as one of those trout he'd eaten.

It was every man for himself. His gelding was going to have to survive on its own.

He'd brought the girls back alive.

She admitted to being surprised.

Well, that wasn't exactly true. She'd expected the man to keep the girls alive or she'd have never let him leave with them. That he'd stayed away so long and managed to get the saddle and bridle off his horse and get the critter turned out to pasture *and* kept the girls alive.

That was the impressive part.

No notion if the man was any good with ranch chores beyond turning his horse loose, but the barn wasn't on fire and that was good enough for Betsy. She had to admit her standards had dropped through the floor since about four days ago when Mark's last hired man had quit and left her to run the place alone. The nasty, selfish varmint.

Mark had left four behind. One had quit because Susie dropped his boots in the water trough. A second had taken to the trail after Annie accidentally let the bull loose, which knocked over the outhouse while he was in it, wearing nothing but long red underwear and those, down around his ankles.

Betsy hadn't seen it, but the final hired man had told her, laughing until he cried.

Then Lilly had wet clean through her diaper while toddling a bit too close to the last cowpoke's lunch pail. He'd grabbed a handful of mane and lit out for California.

Wimps.

Now she had another man in her clutches. She smiled and fluttered her eyelashes. She'd seen her ma give her pa a similar look, and usually Belle got what she wanted when she did it. Of course Ma wasn't pretending, she really did look at Silas in a way that warmed Betsy's heart and made her curious about love.

Now, Betsy had to fake it, but she tried to make it look natural and Matt came on in, sniffing the air. Paying the fluttering lashes no mind but apparently fascinated by the smell of a baking pie.

Fine enough. Betsy would use anything that worked.

"The steaks are ready to take off the fire. I've got fried potatoes ready, and the pie will come out of the oven about the time we're done eating." She fluttered again, just for practice. It was the first meal she'd cooked since she'd taken over. They'd been living on biscuits and milk, and sometimes jerky and water. The family on the trail drive were eating better than she was.

Matt happened to look at her right at that moment. He quit sniffing. He gave her a smile that was like the August sun coming out after a January blizzard. The man must love pie.

Annie picked that moment to jump on a chair and climb onto the table. Matt snatched her just as she prepared to fall face-first onto the platter of hot biscuits.

He made a quick move that settled Lilly in a high chair,

then grabbed Susie as she stumbled and tripped right toward the burning hot stove.

"Emma is going to be so sorry she left these little imps with me when she comes home and finds them all maimed." Betsy's lower lip trembled. She hadn't cried a tear in her life until this week.

"Where are the hands?" Matt sat Susie at the table, and as the four-year-old started to stand, Matt slapped a biscuit in her hands and said, "Sit still, or I'm taking that back."

Susie stayed in place.

Hah! As if that would last.

"I want a biscuit, too!" Annie yowled. Both girls tallied unequal treatment more closely than a miner watches his gold.

"Sit up to the table then." Matt set a biscuit in front of another chair, broke a third one up and put it in front of Lilly as Annie clambered into her chair, and the room went silent.

He looked back at Betsy, who felt her lashes flutter without giving it one thought.

"The hands? It looks like they're behind on the chores."

"The last one quit on Monday."

Matt flinched. "It's Saturday. How long has Mark been gone?"

"Two weeks, and they'll probably be at least three more before they get back."

"Strange time of year for a cattle drive. We drive in October in Texas."

"Fall comes early here and Emma doesn't like cutting it close. She's mindful of the high mountain gaps filling in with an early snow. They normally go later than July, but this is the first one she's gone on for years. She's either been round with a baby or had one mighty young. She loves a cattle drive, though. I convinced her to go and let me watch the girls."

Betsy's lashes fluttered again, completely of their own accord. Matt had come closer, and the girls were feasting. Betsy dropped her voice to a whisper and added, "The stupidest thing I've ever done. I'm not taking good care of the girls. And I'm not taking any care at all of the ranch."

"And the hands all quit?"

Nodding, Betsy said, "Mark left a skeleton crew, four men, plenty to watch what's left of the herd and do daily chores, but two days after he left the steadiest hand broke his arm diving to save Annie when she fell out of the haymow. I'd let her get out of my sight and she'd climbed up there, and Hank saw her in time to catch her."

"Is he here, just laid up?"

Shaking her head, Betsy said, "He saved Annie, but he rammed his head into the barn wall, besides breaking his arm. He was knocked out cold as a mountain peak. They had to take him to Divide to the doctor, and when they got back they said the doctor wants him to stay in bed until he stops seeing two of everything. "I don't know when he'll be back.

"Then the other three quit one at a time. I think if any of them but Travis had been last, they'd have stuck it out rather than abandon me. But Travis was always the least useful of Mark's cowpokes. He gloated when he told me he quit. Then when he rode off and left me he looked back and laughed. The man works with cattle and horses all day. A leaky diaper makes him quit?"

"Betsy, you need help."

She waited for him to say the obvious. He was silent.

Stupid, useless, fluttering lashes.

Not wanting to beg unless she absolutely had to, she rested one open hand on his chest and leaned close so the girls wouldn't start talking and scare him off.

"I need you." She spoke barely above a whisper.

His eyes focused on her words. Or rather her lips, but that was the same thing. He said nothing.

Inching closer, because the situation was dire, she whispered, "So will you help me, Matt? Will you stay? You're going to want to see your brother, aren't you?"

Matt was nodding, watching her. He seemed dazed.

Betsy smiled, and his eyes almost crossed. She gave him a friendly pat on the chest then stepped back, just as his hand whipped out and pulled her close. She bumped right into his chest.

Then as if the impact woke him up, he let her go and took a step back.

Betsy reconsidered the power of fluttering lashes as she whirled to the stove and started scooping up food.

A chair scraped and she glanced back to see Matt sink into it. He looked stunned. She could well imagine. What had happened? She felt like time had stopped and the world had turned soft and beautiful and very private.

Matt felt like he'd been hit with an ax handle.

It took a bit to gather his thoughts, and by then he was eating and no speech was required. When the meal was finished all three girls looked as if their eyelids were drooping. Nap time. Matt knew all about nap time. How he'd hated it for himself.

How he'd loved it for all his whirlwind little brothers.

"For the next two hours we will have peace," Betsy said. "Then it all begins again until night."

"Will you be all right then, in here, while I go fork out the stalls and do a few other chores?"

Betsy, who had ignored him completely while they ate, suddenly looked at him again. Her eyes, so dark brown he could barely see where the pupils began, gleamed with relief and pleasure. "You're really staying then?"

He couldn't do much else. "Yep. Uh. . .you won't let the girls in the creek again, will you?"

Betsy's smile flashed as bright as her eyes. "I handle them fairly well except when I try and do the chores. I just don't have enough hands and eyes. And apparently not enough sense. If you'll do the chores I can take care of the girls."

Matt nodded and pushed back his chair. "I'll get to it then."

He took his Stetson off an antler used as a hook and clamped it on his head and pretty much ran outside.

He'd be fine. . .unless he wanted to eat again. Then things could get confusing.

Chapter 3

Someone pounded the door with the side of their fist. Betsy rose from the chair, the first time she'd been off her feet all day. But whoever was here sounded urgent.

She rushed to the door, flung it open to find Matt, water dripping off his head, right onto Annie, who grinned and revealed a missing tooth.

Betsy was pretty sure the child had all her teeth just an hour ago when she went up to bed.

"How did you get outside?"

Annie jerked one shoulder. Betsy had sounded ferocious, and yet Annie didn't even quit smiling.

"I went out. It's easy." Then she pointed to her mouth. "I lost a tooth, Aunt Betsy."

"And you lost one of your children." Matt looked furious.

His face was red enough the water drenching him might turn to steam at any time.

"I sat with them until they fell asleep. I promise you, I did."

"I believe you." Matt spoke between clenched teeth. He clearly wasn't happy with how this week was going.

Betsy was cooking the best food she could manage, and that was pretty good. Anything to keep from running him off.

"What happened?" Betsy knew that was a stupid question.

"Escaped child. Water trough. Nearly died." Matt growled more than spoke. "Same as every day."

"That's just so true it's almost heartbreaking," Betsy said. "Come in and get changed."

"I'll change in the barn."

"You're freezing. That trough is fed with water from a mountain spring. Run and fetch a change of clothes while I heat up some coffee."

Matt closed his eyes and dragged a deep breath in through blue lips. Betsy appreciated that he was fighting for calm. He'd been sleeping in the bunkhouse all week, and he was doing a fine job of running the ranch. . .for a man without help. She'd tried to help a few times with all three girls at her side. What else could she do but bring them?

"No! Don't even think about helping me." He seemed

to rein himself in when he realized he was shouting. More calmly, he said, "I would appreciate something warm. I'll be right back."

He stood Annie on the floor rather than shove her into Betsy's arms. Which Betsy appreciated. She would have gotten soaked.

Matt stomped away dripping.

Betsy thought she showed great restraint by not snickering. . .until after he was out of earshot.

"Bye-bye, Aunt Betsy." Annie had shed her dress and was on her way out the back door, stark naked. Betsy quit laughing and made a dash to catch the little imp.

Chapter 4

"Another fine meal, Betsy." Matt leaned back from the supper table and patted his stomach—which Betsy couldn't help but notice was flat and hard as a board—even though he put an alarming amount of food away every time she fed him.

All three girls were either asleep or the next thing to it. Matt had moved the baby's tin plate, or she'd be snoring with her face resting in gravy.

"I'll help you get them settled."

"I'm not tired!" Annie wailed. Then her head nodded, jerked up. Susie gave up, crossed her arms on the table, and laid down her weary head.

"Thank you, I'd appreciate it."

Betsy and Matt had learned to work as a decent team.

Matt changed diapers with easy skill. Betsy had the two older girls in their pajamas and tucked in bed by the time Matt had pulled the sleeping gown on Lilly and brought her in. All three girls slept in one room. Mark and Emma shared another. There was a large kitchen with space for a stove and table and sink and some cupboards on one side and a fireplace with a pair of rocking chairs on the other.

It was a tightly built, well-tended home, and when all three girls fell asleep instantly after they laid down, Betsy followed Matt out to those rockers and sank down beside him.

It had become their habit to talk for a few minutes at the end of the day, while they waited to make sure the girls wouldn't stage a prison break.

Matt had nailed the window shut in their bedroom as well as the front door and every other window in the house. The back door was the only way out, so to get out, the girls had to come past Betsy.

The summer nights were cool up here in the mountains, and Matt always laid a fire and started it burning before they ate the evening meal.

By the time the girls were tucked in, it felt good to sit before it for a few minutes. Both of them sighed, such an identical sound that they looked up, and Betsy smiled, then Matt laughed.

She said, "I don't know how Emma does it. I'm sure it helps to have practice, but I spend all day either cooking for them or chasing after them. Lilly can't walk yet, but she crawls so fast and pulls herself up on everything. She scaled a chair and then the kitchen table this morning. She was sitting right on top of the butter dish playing with a butcher knife by the time I got to her."

Betsy shuddered to think of the danger.

Matt shook his head. He took a look at the butcher knife, now hanging from a nail high on the wall, and grinned. "Good spot for it."

"The nail was there. And there's a hole in the knife handle. I suspect that's where Emma keeps it. I just forget all the ways these wily children can find to harm themselves." They shared a look of terror, then both of them laughed.

"How are things outside? Have you cleaned up the mess I made?"

"You couldn't possibly do the outside chores and tend those girls. It wasn't a mess you made, it was you making the right choice and caring for those girls. That's a job that takes all day every day."

Betsy's heart swelled a bit at the kind words. "I think we've almost found everything they can use to kill themselves."

There was an extended silence, broken only by the creak of the rockers. Finally, Matt said, "You're an optimist, aren't you, Betsy?"

They both broke down and laughed hard. It was the closest to a sane adult moment they'd had since they'd met.

"So you've got a herd of little brothers, is that right?" Betsy asked.

"Yep, and one little sister. She's seven years old and that's the last baby Ma had, but Ma is getting up into her forties now. Time for her to slow down with the babies."

Smiling, Betsy said, "I remember all those years I was growing up, Mark telling tales of his family full of boys. Then when your ma had a baby girl, he was so stunned, we thought he'd ride all the way to Texas just to check and make sure they were right."

"I did it."

"What?" Betsy turned away from gazing in the flames to stare at him.

"I went to check. I was in Oregon when I got word, and I rode all the way home. It was just such a shock. I was slow getting there, and Hope was near a year old. And Ma had taken control of the family."

Betsy felt her brow wrinkle. "Taken control how?"

"She made everyone settle down so her baby girl wouldn't be raised in a madhouse. It was a great home to be a growing boy in. A lot of the things we got up to remind me of how Mark's girls act. But the unruly ways of my brothers drove us all away from home at a young age, looking for some peace. Now, well, I thought long and hard about staying down there. My older brothers Abe and Ike are both living near my folks, and I've got several nieces and nephews growing up there. I may wander back down that'a way in the end. I've just never quite got the wanderlust out of my blood."

"Where all have you been?" Betsy sounded wistful to her own ears. "I've never been beyond the state of Montana. In fact, I've barely traveled from here to Divide and Helena. Ma likes to keep us close to home. She doesn't even think her daughters should show themselves in town."

"Why not?"

Betsy shrugged. "Just a habit. The trails are better, and there's a train spur from Divide to Helena now. We can get there in half a day. But when we first settled here we were mighty cut off, and there were a lot of wild men around. Ma didn't like them knowing she had a passel of girls living out in this remote area."

"Well, I've been to near every state in the Union west of the Mississippi. I've never gone back East—except once. I don't know much about city living, but I can survive in the wilderness with a knife and a rifle, don't need any money nor a job. But it's a lonely life. I grew up surrounded by a crowd. I don't last too long on my own before I start longing to hear another voice. I've turned my hand to most every job a man can do. Mining in New Mexico. Lumberjacking in Idaho. I've scouted for the cavalry in Arizona and driven a stagecoach in Colorado. I went to sea in California and sailed all the way around the southern tip of South America. I even landed in New York City, but it was so huge and dirty, I stepped onshore and signed on to a boat sailing back only an hour later. I've seen the Grand Canyon and worked a dozen ranches from Texas to North Dakota. I was even a sheriff in Kansas for a while. I've loved my yondering ways. I reckon I need to settle down one of these days, but it's never stopped being fun to live such a free life."

They talked and rocked late into the night. Betsy knew the morning would come early, with hungry livestock and hungrier girls. But she found herself almost desperate for the quiet adult conversation. It was too sweet to end.

A log split and sent a wash of sparks out of the fireplace. They both jumped up, and Betsy realized how low the fire had burned.

"How long have we been sitting here?" She felt as if the outside world had intruded on something very personal.

Neither of them had a pocket watch, nor was there a clock in the house, but it had to have been more than an hour.

"I reckon I've talked until your ears are aching." Matt gave her his friendly smile, so like the brother-in-law Emma loved so dearly.

They stood, and Matt stepped to the fireplace. "It's a cool night. I'll build up the fire before I go."

"No, it's a tight house. We'll be fine. Thank you." Betsy stood just as Matt turned from the hearth and nearly bumped into her. Matt caught her by the arms to keep from stumbling then was still. His eyes wandered around her face. She felt it like a caress.

He asked, "How did you end up with such shining black curls? Mark told me Emma's hair is whiter than his, and the girls are all so blond."

"Ma married and was widowed. We have different fathers, and Ma says I take after him in looks. My real name at birth was Betsy Santoni; my pa was Italian. But he died when I was a baby, and Ma married Silas. He's the only man I've ever known as my father, and he's a good one and I'm proud to carry his name. My ma said my own pa was pretty worthless."

Matt smiled. "I don't know what kind of man he was, but he must have been good looking to have a daughter as beautiful as you."

Betsy felt something awaken deep in her chest. Something she hadn't known was sleeping. Something she hadn't known was there.

"Thank you." She wondered if she was blushing. She had skin that tanned deeply, and she wasn't given to blushes.

Matt lifted a hand and drew one finger across her cheeks. They must've turned red. . . Why else would he touch her?

"Don't tell me you haven't heard that before. The men in Montana aren't all blind."

Betsy shrugged. "Ma and Pa don't let men come around much."

Matt grinned. "How'd Mark ever get past them?"

"There was trouble and Mark was the right man to help, and somehow, when the trouble passed, he and Emma were planning a wedding. It was fun watching Ma and Pa try'n run him off. And your cousin Charlie was with him, and he ended up married to my sister Sarah."

"I'll have to see Charlie while I'm here, too." Matt's hand opened and rested on her cheek. Quietly, he said, "I don't want to talk about my family anymore."

He leaned down and kissed her.

Her first kiss.

It was his first kiss.

Matt wasn't sure how in the world Betsy Harden had ended up in his arms, but he wasn't going to waste time wondering because it was the best thing that had ever happened to him.

He slid his arms around her waist, his only thought to get closer. He drew her hard against him.

"Matt." She turned her head to break the kiss. Her hands came up to press against his chest. "Wait. Stop."

Her words shocked him into using his head for the first time in a while. He dropped her, only realizing as she slid away that he'd lifted her off her feet.

He stepped back and slammed into the fireplace, which sent him stumbling forward, and somehow, she was right back in his arms. His lips descended, and hers rose to meet him.

The next time they stopped his hands were sunk deep in the dark silk of her hair. He carefully unwound all those lush curls, lingering, kissing her eyes and her blushing cheeks.

She hadn't said "wait" the second time. In fact, her arms were wound tight around his neck. It all added up to her liking this kiss just as much as he did.

This time she stepped back then turned away and breathed deep. "Um. . .you'd better go."

"I want to talk about what just happened here, Betsy. I want it to happen again. I want to have the right to kiss you."

She looked over her shoulder. Her lips were swollen from their kiss. Her hair had tumbled from its bun and flowed wild around her shoulders. She had a little dimple in her chin and her cheekbones were high, her nose strong in a feminine way. He wanted to get to know every bit of her as well as he knew her face.

"What are you saying, Matt? Are you saying you want to court me?"

That wasn't what he was saying. He wanted to marry her and carry her to the bedroom right this minute. And as a man who knew almost nothing about women, he thought he had a great idea of how to proceed.

But courting?

That cleared his thoughts. "Uh, courting. How does a

man even court a woman when he's living with her, eating with her, and raising three children with her? That sounds more like two people who have been married for years." Except of course in one very important way.

His thoughts honestly shocked him a bit because he'd always kept to manly places like the mountaintops and the sea, mining camps and remote ranches. He'd never so much as spent time alone with a woman, not once. Never long enough to consider rounding her up and claiming her.

"Well, nothing like this can happen again as long as we're here alone. It's sinful."

Matt thought it might well be sinful except his intentions, passionate though they were, were completely honorable.

"So you go on now, and when Mark and Emma get back we can talk more about such things as"—kissing, holding, loving? Which would she say?—"courting. Until then, this is improper and a bad example to the girls."

Who were fast asleep and wouldn't know a thing about it.

Matt figured he'd had the only run of luck he was going to get tonight, so he nodded, not agreeing one whit that he needed his big brother around to tell him how to behave, and headed for the door. "I'll see you in the morning for breakfast then, Betsy."

He plucked his Stetson off the hook then turned back to see her watching him, one hand gently touching her lips. Only a will of iron kept him from crossing the room and gathering her right back into his arms.

"Good night." He clamped his hat on his head to keep his hands busy.

"Good night, Matt. I'll see you at breakfast."

Chapter 5

Matt might've just gone whole hog pursuing Betsy Harden if it weren't for those girls, and about a thousand head of cows.

The thunder and lightning in the night had kept Matt from sleep, along with thoughts of beautiful Betsy. As the storm came, Matt felt like he was in the middle of it. Up this high, the clouds sometimes went across the lower slopes of the mountains, below a man. But not this time. The storm was all around him, and sleeping in the bunkhouse, he felt like he was in the middle of a plunging lifeboat at sea.

When the worst passed, he made a dash for the house, worried about Betsy handling the girls. He'd just slammed the door open when the thunder started again.

Only it sounded wrong enough he turned to see hundreds of cattle charging right for him.

He swung the door shut just as a thousand-pound bull leaped up on the porch and ripped the railing away. The animal hit the house so hard it rocked.

A scream behind Matt turned him around to see Annie running for a window, as if she needed to escape. The window was nailed shut and shuttered, but Matt dashed forward and nabbed the little lunatic just as a longhorn rammed its head through, shattering glass and sending shards of wood blasting through the room.

Matt jumped to the side and dropped to the floor, ducking under those horns as fast as he could without crushing Annie. He felt a few sharp slashes, but he missed the worst of it. Then a bellow whipped his head around, and he saw the animal that had busted the window get bunted so hard he came right through, into the room.

Betsy rushed out with a shrieking Susie in her arms. She yelled and grabbed for the broom by the fireplace. She brandished it as the panicked yearling skidded on the split-log floor then fell, jumped to its feet, whirled, and leaped out the same window it'd come in.

The door shuddered under an impact. Matt, still holding Annie, threw his back flat against it. He didn't think he could hold back a charging bull, but if the animal hit the door a glancing blow and Matt kept the door in place, the cattle might not storm inside.

The thundering hooves were deafening.

A wail from the bedroom had a nearly stunned Betsy turning around and rushing in to get Lilly. "Annie, come here to me," Betsy called.

Matt lowered the little girl to the floor. Matt's arms must have seemed like a haven because she turned and jumped back at him.

He hoisted her up, hoping a cow didn't run through the door and crush them both.

Betsy came back, Susie on one hip, Lilly on the other. The noise went on and on.

"The lightning must have spooked them." Betsy spoke load enough to be heard.

Nodding, Matt started thinking beyond survival moment by moment. "How am I going to round them all up?"

"You can't do it alone. We'll have to ride after them."

"We?" Matt looked at how full her hands were. His, too. "We can't take three babies out to herd cattle."

"We can and we will. I don't see as we have much choice. Hopefully they'll calm down and stay mostly together. But if not we'll be combing them out of the trees for ten miles. You can't do that alone."

Matt tried his best to think of something else, but, "You're right. I can't do it by myself. We'll have to let the girls ride with us."

"Emma has a pack she wears so she can strap the baby on her back."

"So one of us wears Lilly?"

"Sure, didn't your ma have something like that?"

"Nope, when we took the wagon to town, the baby sat on her lap until a new one came along, then he joined the brothers in the wagon box."

"Well, we can't hope to herd cattle with a wagon, so we have to ride."

"Listen."

Betsy's eyes lit up. "It's over."

"Almost. They'll tear along for a while, but they'll tire out and calm down."

With a comically arched brow, Betsy said, "That sounds a little like the children."

"A little." Matt grinned as he patted Annie on the back. "The girls never do seem to quite calm down."

They shared a smile, their arms full of children until the last of the thundering hooves faded in the distance.

Betsy realized what else had faded. "The rain and thunder are over."

Nodding, Matt said, "We can't wait until sunrise; who knows how far they'll wander by then. Let's get saddled up."

Chapter 6

W hen Emma asked me to watch her children while she went on the drive I was just plain tickled." The leather of the saddles creaked as they rode along the trail left by the rampaging herd.

Betsy kept up easily, though Matt set a fast pace. They were hoping to catch the cattle before they'd spread far and wide.

Matt had Annie riding in front of him. The little girl's head lolled over Matt's supporting arm. She was deep asleep, as were her sisters.

"I wanted to spend time with my sweet nieces." Betsy gave Susie's tummy a gentle pat. She rode in front and Lilly was on her back.

Matt had wrangled with her, wanting the heavier load,

but Betsy had persuaded him that if there was any hard riding—and there would be—he'd have to do it. Betsy let him think he was the better rider, and maybe he was, but she'd done her share in the saddle and could carry her share of the load.

"And of course the chores would all be done by the hands."

"Those men oughta be horsewhipped for abandoning you."

Nodding, Betsy went on as they rode in the dark. The storm had passed, and the trail, churned up by the cattle, was muddy enough they rode off to the side to avoid the mud as best they could. When the trees got too thick, they were forced to wade through the only existing trail, but when they found open meadows, they could get away from the deep mud. And in those openings, they could see the sky awash in starlight.

If they hadn't been facing hours of grueling work, it might've been nice.

If they hadn't been toting three children, it might've been romantic.

If letting all of Emma's cattle run off wasn't financially ruinous, it might've been fun.

"I thought of it as an adventure. And an honor, honestly. Emma never leaves the girls. She's a fierce, protective mama. So I knew it was a high compliment. Also the cattle drive to Helena is a long, treacherous journey. Even though someone from my family drives cattle every year it's never easy. So Emma must have wanted to get away, have a break from the ranch. I was determined to prove to her she'd done right by trusting me."

"You've kept them alive; no one could dare hope for more."

"So far I've kept them alive. She's not home yet."

Matt smiled, and Betsy realized she could see his face. The gray light of encroaching dawn was pushing back the night. "It was a different kind of adventure than I expected."

"Yep, less like fun and more like a constant battle for survival for all five of us."

Betsy smiled back and spoke the simple truth. "I don't know what I'd have done without you, Matt. I'd have had to abandon all care for the cattle. Which is bad enough without this stampede."

"I'm glad I got here when I did. Betsy, I think, um. . .that is. . .don't you think. . ." The bellow just ahead turned them to face a longhorn bull as he stepped out of a clump of aspen trees, pawing the earth, its ten-foot spread of horns lowered.

"Whoa!" Matt pulled his horse to a stop so suddenly, his gelding reared.

"Go right." Betsy issued the order with a snap then wheeled her horse to the left and raced into the trees. She glanced back to see Matt vanish into the woods on the opposite side of the trail, giving only a moment's thought to the fact that he'd obeyed her so quickly. She'd probably ordered him to do something he was already doing and about to shout at her.

They made a pretty good team.

Betsy put distance between her and that wiry white-and-tan beast, giving the old mossy horn time to calm down as she picked her way through a forest so dense she had no business in it. No trail anywhere. Underbrush between the trees grew until it was almost impenetrable. Bending low to duck branches, letting her horse pick his way through, she headed forward, hoping to get behind the bull and maybe drive him back toward Emma's ranch.

If they could get him moving in the right direction, he would probably just follow his instincts for home. The other cattle might even realize the bull, their natural leader, was gone and follow him.

The practical ranch woman in her doubted it would be that easy.

She thought she'd gone far enough when she heard the lash of a whip. Matt had carried one he'd found in the barn, so he must be working the bull. She headed back for the trail to find the longhorn headed for home, trotting.

Matt heard her emerge from the woods and turned, his alert look telling her that bull had given him all he wanted to handle.

As he rode up, he smiled. "Let's see if we can turn a few more back without getting gored."

"How many cattle were in the herd closest to the house?" Mark and Emma had the cattle spread into several grassy stretches of the high mountains.

"Probably two hundred. I looked before we rode out, and about half are still there. They probably ran a bit to the west and let the thick woods stop them and turn them back. I'd say we're looking for at least a hundred head of cattle."

"So one down, ninety-nine to go?" Betsy sighed. "It's going to be a long day."

The sun peaked over the horizon now, though they were in thick shade. It was finally full light.

"It seemed like a lot more than that when they were crashing around the house last night," Betsy said as they rode on in the direction the cattle had run.

"Well, one bull jumping into the house is a lot." Matt shook his head. "I can't believe there was a longhorn in Mark's house."

Betsy smiled then chuckled. "Emma is going to want us to do some explaining about that."

A small clearing in the woods opened to a couple dozen of the runaway cows. These were docile and their bellies full, so they cooperated nicely and headed down the trail the way they'd come.

"I hope they keep moving, because I'm not going to follow them all the way home." Matt and Betsy sat side by side to watch them disappear down the trail for home.

"You know what else I hope?" Betsy asked.

"What?" Matt reined his horse around and they moved on, following a clear trail that led farther into the woods.

"I hope we catch up with these cows pretty quickly, because I want to get everything in neat order before Emma gets home, or she'll never let me babysit again."

"You mean you want to?" Matt sounded horrified, and Betsy turned, annoyed. He was smiling, laughing at her, and she couldn't help laughing at herself.

The laughter and the sunlight helped wake Susie and Annie up. Lilly slept on as they chased cattle. They got another dozen straggling along the forest path headed back. Then another dozen, then another.

"Another thing I hope. . ." Betsy said when they'd finished with that clearing. Probably seventy-five cows now bound for home.

"What's that?" Matt asked as the woods surrounded them again. Tracks went on even farther from home.

"I hope we find the rest of the cows soon, because if I want to keep this secret we're running out of time." The woods thinned sooner this time, and Betsy saw a few cows ahead. Most likely not all of them, but Betsy decided they'd call this good and give up. They needed to gather what they had and count them, then they could comb the woods for the rest of them over the next few days.

Lilly cried from the pack on Betsy's back.

"We've got to stop. She needs a dry diaper, and I have

some food for all the girls. We're all due to stretch our legs for a bit." Betsy swung down and Matt was just a second slower. Then he stood Annie up on legs that wobbled from riding so long. He led the horses a safe distance away and staked the critters out to graze.

When he came back, he said, "What do you mean by running out of time? We've got as long as it takes."

"I mean we're getting too close to Ma's place."

"Your ma? I thought she went on the cattle drive." Mark led Annie to where Betsy had set out apples and jerky and biscuits. She'd packed well. He could see she'd figured to be all day with this. She changed Lilly's diaper with quick, well-practiced skill.

He doled out the food, and Annie and Susie ate like they were starving, which they most certainly were not.

Betsy sat on the rock with a small cup of milk she'd poured from a canteen and began giving Lilly sips. Matt broke up a biscuit and gave Lilly bites between drinks. He sat beside Betsy, mighty close, since the rock wasn't overly large. He liked the feel of her pressed up to his side.

"Where'd you get an idea like that?"

"I reckon I got it because you were over at Mark's alone. When the last hand ran off, why didn't you load the girls in the wagon and take them to your ma's house to get help?"

Betsy shrugged one shoulder. "It's because my ma raised me and my sisters mostly alone and ran the ranch, too, after the husbands died."

"The husbands? You mean Emma's pa and yours?"

"And one more. Your cousin Charlie is married to my sister Sarah, and she's got a different pa than Emma and I do. She'd buried three husbands before Silas. They were all a worthless lot when they were alive. So she did it all herself.

"I felt like I should be able to handle the girls and the cattle for a few weeks at least. I wanted to prove I could handle whatever trouble I faced. It's because I didn't want to go home, crying for help. And it's worse now than then."

Matt frowned as he slid one arm around Betsy. He was a little hurt. He'd been helping her. "Why's it worse now?"

"Because Ma's not going to like it one bit when she finds out you've been at Emma's with me without an adult chaperone. In fact, she might consider that you've been dishonorable."

"She won't be harsh with you, will she?" Matt was angry at the thought of Belle Harden being wrathful with her daughter. He felt protective. He pulled her closer, the baby still between them but not keeping them far apart.

"I won't let you come to any harm, Betsy." He leaned down and kissed her.

"I'm not worried about me coming to harm, for heaven's sake." She went to push him away and darned if her arm—that wasn't holding Lilly—didn't circle his neck instead and pull him closer.

"You're not? Then what's the matter?" He didn't really

care, not right now. He was too busy kissing this beautiful woman. And enjoying just how enthusiastically she kissed him back.

Betsy broke the kiss but only held herself away a fraction of an inch. "I'm afraid Ma might shoot you on sight."

A chill rushed down his spine at her dead-serious tone. Before he could ask her if she was as serious as she seemed, a crash from the far end of the trail turned his attention. Longhorns plunged out of the woods. The noise was so sudden and startling, that the girls all rushed to Matt's side, and he pulled Betsy close and put an arm around both girls.

Cows kept coming and coming. Probably nearly every one of the unaccounted-for cattle lost in the stampede.

Smiling he looked down and said, "They're all back! We're done with our roundup." He leaned down and kissed her deeply and joyfully.

The sharp crack of a rifle cocking broke the kiss, and he turned to look right down the barrel of a Winchester.

"Get your hands off my daughter."

Chapter 7

Awoman rode straight toward him, her rifle drawn and leveled.

The woman's eyes flashed with golden streaks that a man might mistake for lightning.

Right behind her a man rode, also armed. He was as mad as the bull that'd almost taken them.

Belle and Silas Harden. They didn't look one speck like Betsy, and yet there wasn't a doubt in his mind.

Matt let go of Betsy fast and stepped well away from her. He hoped he lived to tell Mark about how he'd met his in-laws.

The woman's eyes shifted between him and Betsy. Matt figured she didn't miss a thing.

Then he only saw Betsy's back. "Ma, you can't shoot

him, he's Mark's brother."

"That ain't enough to save a man who's got his hands on my daughter."

Betsy's head tilted a bit. "It is if he's got my permission."

The pistol sagged, and Belle Harden didn't look like the kind of woman who ever got careless with a weapon. Then with abrupt, angry motions, she reholstered it. He noticed Silas still had his in hand but pointed in the air.

"He came to visit Mark right after the last hand quit. He saved the girls' lives when they got away from me."

"And why didn't you come to me when that happened?" Belle swung off her horse and ground hitched it. Matt noticed the horse stayed right there, a well-trained critter.

Betsy suddenly broke from where she stood, guarding Matt. . .which had been humiliating, but at the same time he really appreciated it. Leaving Annie and Susie behind, Betsy, with Lilly on her hip, threw an arm around her mother and started crying.

Matt started praying.

He spent a few moments recommitting his soul to the Lord and making sure his spiritual affairs were in order. Because one wrong word from Betsy and he'd be standing at the pearly gates.

Belle didn't shoot, but Silas dismounted and stalked straight for Matt, who scooped both girls up in his arms and said, "Grandpa's here girls. Let's give Grandpa a hug, shall we?"

Both girls yelled with glee. Silas looked frustrated as the girls flung themselves out of Matt's arms and into his. Hard to beat up a man while little girls are hugging you. The look Silas gave him told Matt he was well aware of what Matt was up to. But Silas couldn't resist the little girls and quit trying to burn a hole through Matt with his eyes.

Finally believing he might survive, Matt realized more people were flooding into the canyon. It looked like Belle had found the stray cows and sent up an alarm.

Betsy was babbling something to Belle. It sounded like she was just telling about the cowhands and the trouble. He definitely heard the words, "girls drown" and "Matt came and saved them both."

Which probably wasn't true. The cute little monsters had been fine.

A beautiful redhead rode in, and right behind her was Matt's cousin, Charlie. Charlie would save him. Or Matt would get Charlie killed.

Whichever happened, it was nice to see a familiar face.

A little redheaded boy on Charlie's lap, who looked a lot like the pretty redhead, gave Matt hope. Belle wouldn't shoot her son-in-law's brother, would she?

Matt kept up his praying just to be on the safe side.

Charlie saw him and rode straight over. He dismounted and almost ran, not that easy while wearing cowboy boots, carrying a toddler, and threw his free arm around Matt and pounded him hard on the back, laughing.

He pulled away not knowing he was now a human shield.

"Which one are you?"

Matt had heard that question hundreds of times in his life. It was a fact, he and his many older and younger brothers bore a mighty strong resemblance to one another.

"I'm Matt."

Nodding, Charlie said, "You look so much like Mark I was trying to figure out how he could be here and in Helena at the same time."

"I'm so much better looking than Mark it ain't even funny."

Charlie started laughing. "And is it true that your ma had a girl?"

"Yep. Pa's thirteenth child was finally a girl."

"Twleve sons?" Belle exclaimed. "And your ma didn't lose her mind or take after your pa with a skillet?"

Betsy turned to Matt. "Ma's always been fond of her girls."

Belle was now holding Lilly, which made her seem far less dangerous.

Silas came up beside Belle. "You're fond of your sons,

too, aren't you, honey?"

"That I am, Silas. Right fond of the sons we've made." Belle gave Silas such a warm look Matt was almost dazed.

A young man caught up with Belle and stood beside her, grinning. "I've taught you how good it can be to have a boy, haven't I, Ma? Me and my four brothers?"

"This is my little brother, Tanner." Betsy pointed to another barely grown boy. "And that's Si. The rest of the boys went on the cattle drive with Mark."

Tanner was as tall as Silas and had his ma's hazel eyes, and skin that was as tan as an Indian. Si was probably Silas Jr. He took after his pa, though both the parents were brown haired, so the resemblance between them was strong in general coloring.

Charlie shook his head. "It was all we could do to stop Mark from riding for Texas when he got word about a baby sister. He figured a terrible mistake had been made, and if it hadn't, he was scared for his little brothers."

"Most of us got home to see if it was true. Ike's moved home permanently and married Laura McClellen."

"I hadn't heard that." Charlie's eyes lit up. He looked at Belle. "Laura McClellen is Mandy Linscott's baby sister."

"Sophie McClellen ended up with a Reeves in her family, too?" Belle looked glum.

The pretty redhead plucked her little boy out of Charlie's arms.

"Why is my sister crying? Betsy never cries." Less

friendly than Charlie by a country mile. Matt remembered her name was Sarah. Betsy had mentioned her plenty of times since he'd gotten here.

Charlie looked from Matt to Sarah to Betsy. His brow lowered with worry, and he rested a hand affectionately on Sarah's back. "We found Mark's cattle coming onto our property. Figured the storm stampeded them. I sent word there was trouble, which brought Belle and Silas and a passel of others. How long have you been living with Betsy?" Charlie choked over that and cleared his throat and said, "I mean uh. . .how long have you been sleeping together at Mark's place. . .no, I mean—"

Matt kicked Charlie in the ankle, and he didn't even care that everyone saw it. "Stop talking before you get me killed."

There was a long silence. Charlie looked to be thinking of what to say and discarding many possible choices. Finally, he raised his hands as if surrendering and said rather weakly, "Welcome to Montana, Matt."

If this was how a man got welcomed to Montana, it was no wonder the state was mostly empty.

"Let's get these cattle home, then we'll settle this." Silas took charge, which seemed mighty brave for some reason. It stood to reason the man of the family would take charge, and yet there was something about Belle that said no one took charge of her, ever. Matt would bet she wasn't a tractable kind of wife. Love and honor, sure, if she deemed a man worthy.

Obey…most likely she'd only do that if she was ordered to do something she planned to do anyway.

But Silas looked like a man who knew ranching, which Belle most likely respected, so her going along with him, well, if a body wanted to call that obedient they were welcome to do so.

A couple of the hands went on ahead. The rest of the hands, along with Betsy's two little brothers, hazed the critters in the clearing toward the trail and fell in behind them.

The cattle were tired from a long run, and their bellies were full of lush grass. It had turned them into purely docile critters.

The Harden family—and Matt—brought up the rear. They were on the way to Mark's in a matter of minutes.

But the trail was barely wide enough to ride two abreast, and Belle led the family group with Betsy at her side and Lilly strapped on her back. Betsy had Susie in front of her.

Silas was next, riding side by side with Sarah. Silas had Annie.

Matt found himself at the end of the line with Charlie, and Charlie's son riding on his pa's lap. The riding arrangements didn't suit Matt at all. He needed to talk to Betsy, and he knew about decent behavior, so he needed to set things right by having a talk with Betsy's pa about his intentions. . .even though he hadn't exactly had time to figure out what his intentions were.

As they rode, Matt thought that no two girls ever looked less like their ma than black-haired, black-eyed Betsy and green-eyed redheaded Sarah.

Matt leaned close to Charlie and whispered, "Do you have any control over your wife?"

Charlie grinned. "Not mostly."

"Can you get her back here so I can have a talk with Betsy's pa?"

Charlie's eyes went wide. Fear, plain and simple. "I've done that before. It ain't an easy talk." Then Charlie, who'd always been Matt's favorite cousin, said, "Welcome to the family."

Much like his welcome to Montana. Charlie was just full of interesting ways to greet a man. And then he proved to have another one. He looked down at his boy, whose name Matt hadn't even asked yet, and patted the tyke affectionately on the tummy.

"Sarah," he spoke so his voice carried to his wife, "I haven't fed the baby in a while. You have some biscuits we could feed him, don't you?"

Sarah went from ignoring Matt and talking quietly with her pa to looking down at her son with concerned maternal eyes.

She dropped back, and Matt didn't waste a moment urging his horse ahead to take Sarah's place. He saw

Charlie grab his wife's reins when she tried to block Matt. Then Matt was there and Silas turned the coldest blue eyes on Matt he'd ever seen.

Well, Matt was no boy, nor was he a coward. He'd spent time kissing Betsy, and as an honorable man, who wanted leave to kiss Betsy any time he wanted, he didn't hesitate to do what was right.

Chapter 8

"Elizabeth Harden, what were you thinking?" Belle set a brisk pace, and Betsy had the sense her ma was trying to leave Matt in the dust.

Since Matt was riding along with Charlie, who knew the way, Betsy didn't figure they'd lose him.

Every time her ma called her Elizabeth, it sent a chill down Betsy's spine, because trouble always followed.

Well, Betsy was past the age of getting a hiding, and Ma had never been one to hand out her punishments in that harsh way.

But on the other hand, there was never any doubt that making Ma mad was going to be followed with long, deep regrets.

"Why didn't you just load up the girls and come

home? We'd have helped."Then Ma's expression changed from anger to something else. Something soft and sad, as if she was hurt. Her pain was a lot harder to take than anger.

"Have I ever acted as if you can't come to me for help, Betsy? You know I'll always come a-runnin' if you need me. I haven't acted as if you can't, have I?"

"No, Ma." Betsy reached across and gave her ma's arm a squeeze. "It's because I knew you'd come that I didn't ask. I wanted to prove I was up to handling everything. I've heard the stories of you taking care of our whole ranch with no man. I felt like a failure because I wasn't up to it. I kept meaning to just come for you, but then I'd think I could just get through one more day, prove to myself. . .and you and Pa, that you'd raised me right."

"Betsy, you're as smart and hardworking as the day is long. You don't have to prove a single thing to me because I've seen plenty of proof over the years."

Letting go of her ma's arm, Betsy smiled, but inside she couldn't help feeling the twist of failure. "But you did it, Ma. Why couldn't I? Because I was sure enough failing at it. And if Matt hadn't come. . ." She thought of that fast-moving creek, and a cold chill raised goose bumps on her arms. "Matt saved the girls' lives, Ma. They'd slipped away while I did chores, thinking they were napping. If he hadn't been there. . ." Shaking her head she couldn't control a shudder.

"But you shouldn't have been kissing a man you'd only met days ago."

A long silence followed. Betsy glanced back and saw that Matt was now riding alongside Pa and Sarah had dropped back and was fussing with her baby. Betsy said a quick prayer to God to protect Matt from Pa.

Leaning close to Ma, she spoke so her voice wouldn't be heard. "How long did you know Pa before you kissed him the first time?"

Another long silence. Then Ma said, "Don't try and change the subject. I've told you before that a man can't be trusted. You know better'n to—"

"How long, Ma?" Betsy knew her ma real well, and she knew when a question was being dodged.

"Anthony, your pa, came around for weeks before I—"

"I'm talking about Silas, and what's more, you know it. He's the only man I call Pa."

Ma glared at Betsy, who'd been raised to be tough, even with her own mother.

Betsy arched her brows and stared right back, maybe not so ferociously as Ma, but then Betsy wasn't half trying.

Finally Ma looked away. "When we first kissed isn't the point. We'd known each other through a long, hard cattle drive. I knew the kind of man he was. I respected—"

"That fast, huh?" Betsy smiled then snickered. "Why Belle Tanner Harden, you scamp. I think the two of us need to compare our history and just see which of us is better behaved around men."

Ma's eyes narrowed, then after a few seconds she rolled them toward heaven and said, "Our first kiss came too fast."

"I'm sure mine and Matt's did, too. But it was only a kiss. He treated me with honor; he worked hard outside, slept in the bunkhouse every night, and helped with the girls as well. He's got a passel of little brothers, and he's as good with children as I am, maybe better because by his own admission he was as much of a scamp as Mark growing up."

"No one can be as much of a scamp as Mark." Ma didn't admit it often, but Betsy knew she was right fond of her son-in-law, and Emma was still very much in love with her husband.

"That's true. But Matt seemed to keep ahead of the girls as if he'd seen it all before."

Ma glanced back then looked quickly away. "You're sounding like you're pretty serious about this young man. Just because he's Mark's brother doesn't mean you really know him. You need time to learn if he's an honest, God-fearing man who will be dependable over the years."

"I agree. I like him real well, but I'm going to spend time getting to know him better. I can promise you I'm not going to be rushed into anything with a near stranger."

"Belle." Pa had closed the distance between himself and Ma.

"Yes, Silas?" Ma looked as if she wanted to keep pestering Betsy.

"Matt just asked for Betsy's hand in marriage. He wants to ride straight into Divide and have the wedding today."

Chapter 9

Betsy started coughing.

They emerged from the woods with only a wide pasture ahead of them before they reached Mark's house.

Matt rode past Silas and brought his horse right up beside Betsy—on the side away from Belle. He patted her on the back until she recovered.

"I wanted to talk with you about it first, honey." He gave Silas a narrow-eyed look for being so blunt. His soon-to-be father-in-law. . .if Matt handled all this right. . . looked completely unrepentant.

Now here he was with Silas and Belle watching his every move, and Charlie and Sarah close enough to have heard everything—and riding in closer. And Betsy looking like she wanted to make a run for it.

"Give your horse to your pa and let's walk together the rest of the way."

"You're not going anywhere alone with my daughter," Belle snapped.

Matt knew good and well that before this was over he was going everywhere with Betsy Harden. He let that thought keep him from growling.

Instead he dismounted and plucked Betsy off her horse. "Watch us. Listen to me talk then, Belle. But Betsy deserves to hear some nice words about how wonderful I think she is. And she needs to hear. . ." Matt looked away from Belle and talked to pretty Betsy.

". . .you need to hear that I want the right to kiss you anytime I choose. I want to spend my life with you, Betsy. You're the prettiest woman I've ever seen. The prettiest I've ever imagined."

Matt realized that the crowd was gone. They were probably disgusted, but maybe they also had a little shame. For whatever reason, the family had ridden on for the ranch house, Charlie leading both Matt's and Betsy's horses.

"But that's not why I want to join my life with you. I can see your goodness, and I respect your toughness and your fine heart and sharp mind. I would be the luckiest man in the world to have you marry me. You're the kind of woman a man would want to have by his side to weather life's storms like last night, and to enjoy during the good times."

Betsy honestly wanted to say yes, but he'd yet to say the one thing that would matter, and what's more, he couldn't say it. They'd been through a hard spell together. She'd seen how he handled trouble. But that wasn't enough for her. She wanted what she saw pass between Ma and Pa. Between Mark and Emma, Charlie and Sarah.

"I know you're a practical woman, Betsy. So I've given you practical reasons why you should marry me. But the real reason I'm asking is, I've fallen in love with you. Now I don't reckon—"

Betsy threw herself into his arms and kissed him before he could say something that would make a hash out of the beautiful words. Matt's arms came around her waist; he lifted her straight off her feet. Then he whirled her in a circle and broke the kiss to laugh out loud with joy.

When the celebration ended, Matt eased her away from him. "I'm taking that for a yes, but I'd like to hear the words."

"Yes, I'll marry you, Matt. And I'll consider myself the luckiest woman on earth."

They were awhile speaking again, then Betsy pulled away and said, "Let's go on and catch up with the others."

Her family had to have settled the cattle in by now. So they'd be waiting at Emma's house.

Nodding, Matt looked at her for too long, and Betsy

had never felt so wanted, so loved. Not in a man and woman kind of way.

"Let's go." He slid his arm around her waist and they walked toward the ranch house, a hundred yards away.

Chapter 10

Five riders approached the cabin as Matt neared it. His spirits rose—and that was sayin' something because they were already sky-high. One of those riders was his brother.

"Mark's home. That must be Emma at his side."

"Yep, we made it. We kept all three girls alive."

Matt chuckled, then he laughed, and Betsy laughed along with him until the two were nearly limp.

They were calming down when they reached the house. Mark had gone inside, but he came running out looking around. His eyes landed on Matt.

"Matt!" His big brother rushed to him, and they grabbed each other. Matt was shocked at how nice it was to see someone from his own family. He had one terrible moment when a burn of tears washed over his eyes. He fought them off and hung on to Mark, pounding his back and laughing.

Mark finally backed up and dashed his wrist across his eyes, but Matt saw what just might have been tears. He'd have tormented Mark about it if that wouldn't have made him a hypocrite.

"It is good to see someone from home, little brother." Then Mark turned to Betsy. "And I was inside long enough to hear my brother was asking you to marry him."

The smile that broke out on Mark's face helped Matt to make some decisions on the spot. The main one being he'd find a way to stay in this area, because he'd been considering taking Betsy on his wandering with him while they hunted for a place to settle. Maybe taking her home to Texas. But having Betsy's family nearby, and Matt having his brother and cousin, was too tempting to resist.

Betsy's smile was as wide as Mark's. "Yep, we're getting married."

"We didn't talk about when." Matt took Betsy's hand. "But I'd like to see to it right away."

He met Betsy's eyes, and she nodded. "As soon as we can hunt up a parson."

Matt took her hand and threaded his fingers between hers. "That suits me just fine."

"I now pronounce you man and wife." Parson Red Dawson smiled as he closed his prayer book. "You may kiss the bride."

Matt turned to Betsy, humbled and thrilled to have gotten such a treasure for a wife. The kiss was quick and sweet, a completely appropriate kiss for two people standing before a throng of family and friends.

They faced the gathering, then Matt took Betsy's hand and hooked it through his elbow and they marched down the aisle formed by their wedding guests.

He was outside and surrounded by well-wishers when he saw a familiar face. "Mandy McClellen?"

"Matt!" Mandy took both his hands, smiling so big it was blinding. "Have you been home lately? Have you seen Laura since she married Ike?"

The two chattered together a long while. Matt loved seeing another face from home. Since Matt had been home recently, Mandy was full of questions about her sister Beth, not to mention her other sister Laura who'd married Matt and Mark's brother Ike. Mandy quizzed him until he'd told everything he knew.

Then a tall blond man dragged Mandy's hands away from Matt.

"Oh, Matt. My husband, Tom Linscott. Tom, this is Mark Reeves's brother. He's got another brother, Ike, married to my little sister Laura. You remember when I got word Laura was married?"

Matt saw clear as day that Tom Linscott hadn't liked another man holding his wife's hands. But he must have trusted his wife—he'd have been a fool not to. Mandy was the most upright fussbudget Matt had ever known. Mark especially had lived to torment her when they were kids— and Matt had helped all he could.

Belle joined them, her hazel eyes serious, stern, worried. Well, Matt would ease her worries by being the best husband a woman ever had. But it would take time to prove all that to Belle.

"We've all brought potluck," Belle said. "We can have a feast."

Silas was behind his wife. "I've got a stretch of land for you, Matt. It's a nice high valley that will be close to Charlie and Mark and close up the distance between us and our Lindsay. I've a mind to own every inch of the trail to Helena before I'm done. And with all our boys," Silas slid his arm behind Belle's waist and smiled down at her, "I think we can do it, don't you, honey?"

Since Matt was determined to make his wife happy and living next to Mark suited him, he nodded as Silas Harden arranged his life.

Charlie came up as soon as there was a break in the hand shaking and back slapping. "I've got a line shack near my place. I sent my men out there to make sure it's clean and stocked with food and to set it up so you can have privacy.

A wave of dizziness came over Matt to think of the wedding night ahead.

Mark was right behind Charlie. "Trust me, Matt, you don't want to stay overnight at your in-laws' house on your wedding night."

Matt had himself a wife, and he wanted to be with her, as a man was with a wife.

"I'll tell Betsy. I didn't figure I was ever gonna be alone with her." Frowning, he added, "It sounds like Silas is going to tell me where to live and build me a house and give me some cattle. He doesn't have to do that. I have some money saved up, and I'm not afraid of hard work."

"He did that for me," Mark said. "It was like standing in front of an avalanche. I tried to tell him I could take care of my own wife, but he wouldn't hear of not helping me get set up. The whole Harden clan is crazy to protect their daughters. Belle's first husband left her to do everything on her own. I guess this is their way of not letting that happen to their girls. And it made Emma happy, as well as making our first years together much more comfortable."

Matt looked at Charlie. "You and Sarah, too?"

Charlie nodded, "Yep, 'tweren't no stopping him. And when I protested I was a little bit afraid Belle was going to shoot me, so I just gave them what they wanted."

"Anyway, the land he's speaking of is a beautiful place. And not too far from here."

They'd gotten married at Mark's place.

Mark slapped Matt's shoulder. "I'm glad to have some more family close by. Charlie and I have been treated real well by the Hardens, but to watch them all be a close family makes me lonely for more of my own brothers. I'd love to see Ma and Pa, too. I might do it now that you're close. Emma and I could ride to Texas, catch a train part of the way, and leave the girls here with you and Betsy."

"That's not going to happen, Mark." Betsy's horrified voice turned them to face her. "You take them with you if you want to go to Texas."

"I can't. Ma and Pa are snowed in during the winter, and there's too much work during the summer."

"They're not snowed in anymore. Ma made Pa dynamite the opening so it's wider. They come and go all winter long now."

Mark gasped. "How'd she get him to do that?"

"There've been a lot of changes since that baby girl was born."

"I'd heard there were, but I never dreamed they'd blasted the canyon entrance."

"Yep, the little brothers never miss school, either."

"They must hate that."

"Not really. Ma brought order to the whole house, and the boys behave well at school, too. It's shocking at first, but you get used to it. But even if you couldn't go in the winter, we wouldn't watch your young'uns." Matt went to his wife and slid his arm around her waist. "Your daughters are more than we can handle, Mark. You take 'em with you, or you don't go."

Emma said quietly, "I noticed the bars on the windows." She glanced at Mark and smiled. "Why didn't we think of that?"

"Besides," Matt went on, "Ma will want to see her grandchildren." Matt looked down at Betsy, who was smiling at him, probably grateful that he was saving her from Mark's daughters.

Nope, he sure as shootin' didn't want to spend his wedding night with his in-laws.

"Let's go saddle up, wife. Charlie has cleaned up a line shack for us. We can commence to having our honeymoon as soon as we get there." Just saying it out loud made Matt's head spin. He urged Betsy toward the horses.

"Pa wants to help build us a house, but he'll wait until tomorrow." Betsy smiled and leaned against him then she lifted her right hand to show him the satchel she carried. "Tonight we're on our own, and I'm ready to go."

Epilogue

The peace of a new beginning washed over him as they said their good-byes and walked toward their horses together.

The line shack wasn't far, but far enough. When they came to the front door, Matt dropped the satchel and swept Betsy up into his arms.

"I've heard of a tradition, Mrs. Reeves. It's supposed to bring good luck to a marriage if the groom carries the bride over the threshold of their first home."

Betsy gave him a teasing smile and reached down to open the door of the tiny one room cabin. "Good luck brought by such means smacks of superstition, Mr. Reeves. And I don't hold with such things."

"Neither do I, Betsy darlin'. But your ma gave me

such an evil look when I told her we were leaving the party, I think I can use all the luck I can get. And the protecting hand of God, too."

Betsy laughed. "Carry me in then, and you can carry me into our home, too, when Pa gets it built."

"That will be my pleasure. Any excuse to hold you close." Matt walked inside, and Betsy gasped.

"Did Charlie do this?" The room was filled with wild-flowers, and the scent of them made the little cabin homey and welcoming. A pot of stew simmered on the stove, adding to the pleasant aroma.

"He said he sent some of his hired men over to bring bedding and food. I'm betting your sister thought of the flowers. That ain't Charlie's style."

Betsy laughed.

Matt stood Betsy on her feet and closed the door, shutting out the world.

"I have myself a wife who is tough and smart and sweet and kind. The prettiest woman I've ever imagined. I can't wait to get on with being a husband who is worthy of you."

"You know, Matt, even though I spent most of the last week inside, I really am used to helping outside. I know horses and cattle. I understand mountain grazing and treacherous trails. I'm going to be a partner to you in this ranch."

"So I've got me a bride who rides herd, huh?"

"You do indeed."

Matt kissed her soundly and got on with being a husband in the most wonderful way of all.

Mary Connealy writes romantic comedy with cowboys. She is a Carol Award winner, and a Rita, Christy, and Inspirational Reader's Choice finalist. She is the bestselling author of the *Wild at Heart* series, *Trouble in Texas* series, *Kincaid Bride* series, *Lassoed in Texas* trilogy, *Montana Marriages* trilogy, *Sophie's Daughters* trilogy, and many other books. Mary is married to a Nebraska cattleman and has four grown daughters and a little bevy of spectacular grandchildren. Find Mary online at www.maryconnealy.com.

BLUE MOON
BRIDE

Susan Page Davis

Chapter 1

Ava Neal's younger sister burst into her bed-chamber.

"Ava!" Sarah hurried across the room as quickly as her long rose-colored taffeta dress and her fashionable shoes would allow. "Conrad has proposed. We're getting married."

Ava pulled her into a fierce hug. "Oh, my dear! I'm so happy for you."

"Really?" Sarah drew away and eyed her critically. "Are you sure?"

"Of course. Why wouldn't I be? Conrad is a fine young man, and he obviously adores you. He'll make you a wonderful husband."

"Well, we always thought you'd be the first down the aisle."

"True, but we Neal sisters are unconventional, aren't we? We've never set much store by what people think."

"You're not crying, are you?" Sarah asked.

"No! Well, perhaps." Ava chuckled and swiped at a tear escaping down her cheek. "But these are happy tears, I assure you."

"They're not"—Sarah studied her with an anxious frown—"not because of Will Sandford?"

"Of course not! That was long ago."

"Yes."

Ava grasped her sister's hand. "You've told Mama and Pa, of course."

"We did, and they seem quite pleased about it. They asked me to run up and get you. You'll join us, won't you?"

"I certainly will."

Ava steered Sarah out to the landing and down the stairs to the parlor. The more people the merrier just now, and if anyone else alluded to her state of singleness at the age of twenty-two, or to her heart being broken when Will Sandford died, she would ignore them.

At the parlor door, she allowed Sarah to draw her in and over to Conrad's chair. He stood, blushing a little, as Ava laid her hand on his sleeve.

"Conrad, Sarah has told me the good news. I am so pleased."

"Thank you." He let her draw him down for a kiss on his cheek, which made him flush even deeper.

"Sit down, girls," her mother said. "I've made fresh tea."

Mama had also brought out the macaroons and ginger gems they had baked that afternoon. Mama always had some confection on hand when her daughters received gentleman callers.

"Let me help you." As usual, Ava served while her mother poured the tea. They had developed the routine years ago, without discussing it. She gave Conrad the first cup, then Sarah, and then her father. While Mama poured for Ava and herself, Ava passed the pressed-glass plate of cookies.

At last, she settled on a chair near her father.

"Have you discussed a date between you?" Mama asked Sarah.

"A little." Sarah glanced at Conrad. "We thought we'd like to have it in June if we can, though time is short."

"Of course, a June bride." Mama's smile belied any difficulty in organizing a wedding in less than six weeks.

Ava sipped her tea and let the talk flow around her. Conrad must have approached her father sometime during the day, probably at Pa's office in town. He had obviously received permission to offer Sarah his hand, as Pa now seemed perfectly contented with the way things were going.

Ava tried not to imagine how different things would be now if she were the one being courted, or if she were now a married woman and could host a party for Sarah in her own home.

She was only fifteen when Will went off to war, and sixteen when they'd heard he'd been killed. Some had supposed she was too young to truly know love, but her family understood how the news shattered her. Ava often thought that, because she was so young, those feelings had faded more slowly than they would have in an older woman.

"And you'll need a new gown, Ava," her mother said, jerking her back into the present.

"Wh— Oh, for the wedding?"

"Of course, darling," Sarah said. "You will stand up with me, won't you?"

"If you wish it."

"I wouldn't have anyone else." Sarah reached over to squeeze her hand. "I was thinking pale blue watered silk. Or would you prefer green?"

"Whatever you decide on," Ava said. No one would ever suggest she wear pink or burgundy, with her auburn hair. She could trust Sarah's judgment there.

"Perhaps you ladies should go to the shops tomorrow and see what they have laid in," her father suggested.

Ava looked at him in surprise. Pa was in a generous mood this evening. He must truly be happy with Sarah's choice. Perhaps he was relieved that he would have one less eligible daughter to worry about.

"What a splendid idea," Mama said. "We'll make a day of it and eat luncheon in town. Now, Conrad, do your parents know?"

The corners of Conrad's mouth quirked, and he glanced at Sarah. "Well, I did drop a hint to them before I left the house. They seemed quite agreeable. My mother told me to ask if Sarah may join us for dinner Sunday."

"Of course," Mama said. "And we'll want to have your whole family over soon. Maybe next week."

Ava realized her father was watching her, not the prospective bride. He gave her a gentle smile.

"Ava, would you mind refreshing that tea? I think we need another pot."

"Of course, Pa." Ava rose and took the nearly empty teapot off the serving table.

A moment later, her father followed her into the kitchen.

"All right, kitten?"

"I'm fine, Pa." She measured the dried tea leaves into the infuser and placed it in the teapot.

"Right." He stood there watching her work.

"What?" Ava asked.

"Memories waylay us at the most inconvenient times."

She grimaced. "I hoped it wasn't obvious."

"Not too badly."

"I'm truly happy for Sarah and Conrad."

"I'm sure," her father said. "That doesn't make it easier, though."

Ava sighed and turned to the stove for the teakettle. "I thought maybe I'd do some traveling this summer, Pa.

After the wedding, of course. I wouldn't leave before then."

"Travel where?"

"I'd just like to get away. Maybe have a little adventure of my own." A thought came to her, and she glanced up at him. "I could go out and visit Polly Tierney."

Her father blinked, frowning a little. "Polly? Kitten, she lives clear out in the Wyoming Territory."

"Well, yes, but it's civilized now, or nearly so. And travel is so much easier out there, now that they have railroads clear across. I could take a train to Cheyenne. Polly and Jacob could fetch me there."

"I don't know..."

Ava poured the boiling water into the teapot. "Please, Pa? It would give me something to look forward to after the wedding."

"Maybe so. I'll mention it to your mother tonight. Start her thinking about it a little."

Ava laughed. "I doubt you can get her to think about much besides wedding plans right now, but it wouldn't hurt to plant the idea in her mind."

Joe Logan sat in the waiting room at Becker and Fixx, Attorneys at Law, and doodled on the edge of the newspaper he'd picked up. He hated waiting, and his fingers always reached for a pencil when he had to sit for a while.

The front page of the paper had a story about the

devastating effects of a recent hurricane on Labrador, and another on outlaw Jesse James's latest escapades out west. Joe sketched a man on horseback, his face obscured by a knotted handkerchief, riding with a pistol in his outstretched hand. Not bad. Joe still thought he might be able to find a place as an illustrator, but he'd probably have to go to New York for that, and rumors said the price of food and lodging there was outrageous.

A bell sounded briefly from the next room, and the secretary who sat at a desk across the room looked at him. "Mr. Becker will see you now."

Joe brushed a bit of dust from his jacket and fingered the tie knotted around his neck before entering the inner office. Mr. Becker was particular about his employees' appearance.

"There you are, Logan. I have a job for you if you want it. It's a bit more involved than the jobs I've given you before."

Mr. Becker nodded toward an empty chair, and Joe sat down.

"That's fine, sir." Joe would like having more regular income, but he hadn't been able to secure a steady position since his old employer had died in November, leaving him at loose ends. The courier jobs and errands he performed for Hartford businessmen barely paid his living expenses.

The attorney sat back and studied him for a moment. "I've a client who doesn't trust the postal service, and he wants a packet hand-delivered."

Joe nodded, glad it wasn't a summons to serve a court witness. He always found that task distasteful. "Is it documents, sir?"

"Er, no. The gentleman was recently widowed, and he wants to send a few of his wife's bits to their daughter. She's married and living in San Francisco."

Joe tried not to let his excitement show in his face. He had never set foot west of the Appalachians. San Francisco, and all expenses paid. Those "bits" must be valuable.

"You'll need to get some signatures, too. I sent some papers in January, and the daughter claims she signed them and sent them back, but they never arrived here." Becker shook his head. "You just can't rely on the mail west of the Mississippi, I'm afraid. So you'll take the papers out and have her sign them when you give her the jewelry, and then you'll bring the documents back."

It sounded simple enough. "When do you want me to leave, sir?"

"Soon. I'll have Mr. Franklin see to your railroad ticket. Next week, I suppose. End of the month. You'll have a berth on the train, but you'll have to find a hotel once you arrive. I don't expect it will take you more than a day or two to take care of your errand, and then you must head right back."

Joe nodded. Surely somewhere in there he could squeeze out a few hours to enjoy seeing San Francisco. It might as well be Paris—distant, exotic. He could hardly wait.

"You will wire me when you have completed the delivery," Mr. Becker went on.

"Yes, sir." That would, of course, be his first order of business when he got to San Francisco.

"We will advance you money for your expenses and pay you fifty dollars upon your return. Is that acceptable?"

To Joe, it was very acceptable. The trip would take him less than a month—perhaps much less, and he fully expected to enjoy himself.

"Perfectly," he said.

"All right. See Mr. Franklin at the front desk. Come 'round to get your ticket the morning before your departure, and we'll give you the client's packet."

"Very good, sir."

"And Logan, if this goes well—that is, if you successfully deliver this parcel—why, we might have regular daily employment for you on your return. Are you interested?"

"Oh, yes, sir. Thank you." Joe left the office whistling and went back to his boardinghouse. Unfortunately, he would probably have to pay for his room in advance, or the landlady would let it out to someone else in his absence, but overall, he felt good about the prospect of this new venture.

After dinner, he went down to the parlor to save burning his own lamp oil. He found a quiet corner where the other boarders would hardly notice him and opened his drawing tablet. He had splurged on it a couple of months ago, but it was full now, and he had to flip through it before he found a page with enough empty space for him to draw a locomotive spurting smoke. San Francisco! He would most definitely have to buy a new sketchbook before he embarked.

Chapter 2

SAFELY ACROSS MISSISSIPPI

A va reread her brief message. Mama would fuss about the unnecessary expense if she added much more. She would save her descriptions of the journey until she had a chance to write a full letter. Still, her parents would be waiting fretfully for news, especially Mama.

So far, the railroad journey had been interesting, especially after they left New England and passed through vast tracts of forest and farmland. As yet there was no bridge across the river at St. Louis, though one apparently was planned, and Ava had joined her fellow passengers on a ferry ride over the roiling waters of the Mississippi. Seeing the mighty river, the barges of coal and wheat, and the steamboats plying up and down the channel had thrilled her. Thanks to the modern wonder of the submerged telegraph cable, her parents would receive her message before suppertime.

While the porters transferred the baggage from the ferry to a wagon, the passengers drifted toward the eateries near the waterfront. They had an hour before their next train would board, and most of the travelers hoped to find a decent meal in the interval. Ava found a lunch counter that served soup and sandwiches. When she gave her order, she asked for a packet of extra sandwiches to take with her.

She entered the railroad car before most of the other passengers and found a window seat two rows back from the vestibule. Last week, she and her father had engaged in quite a discussion on the merits of window seats versus aisle seats. Her mother, on the other hand, seemed only to be fretting about the impression a young woman traveling alone would give. As the others entered and claimed places, Ava tucked her handbag and sandwiches between herself and the wall and peered out the window at the flurry of activity on the platform.

"Pardon me. Is this seat taken?"

She looked up into the keen blue eyes of a young man, clean shaven and of respectable dress, who stood in the aisle, his derby hat in one hand and a small leather valise in the other.

"Not at all." Ava's lips curved—not too encouraging, she hoped. Mama had been quite expansive about the encouragement young men might take from a winsome smile.

She tried not to look at him as he settled in, but she noted that after placing his hat on the rack overhead, he slid his leather case beneath the seat and kept the heel of his shoe nestled against it when he sat down, as though he didn't want to lose track of that case for a second.

The car filled rapidly, and the conductor passed through. Two gentlemen arrived separately and claimed the seats opposite them, offering the perfunctory greetings of strangers. The train started with a lurch and then a steadily increasing rumble. Ava was getting used to the sounds and rhythms of the rails, and she felt like quite a seasoned traveler now. One of the men across from her opened a newspaper, and the other leaned back and closed his eyes. Ava studiously gazed at the shifting landscape outside.

When the conductor came to check their tickets, the young man leaned back and allowed her to present hers first.

"We'll reach Cheyenne late tomorrow morning, miss." The conductor tore off a portion and handed her the stub.

The young man gave him his ticket, and the conductor nodded. "And you've got quite a trip still ahead of you, sir. You should arrive Wednesday morning, 11:15. Independence Day."

"So it is," the young man said. "I expect they'll have some doings in San Francisco?"

"I shouldn't wonder." The conductor gave him his ticket stub. "Let me know if you folks need anything."

When he had moved on, the young man turned to Ava. "I'm Joseph Logan, by the way."

"How do you do? Ava Neal." She held out her gloved hand, and he grasped it briefly.

"I admit I'm curious," he said. "What draws you to Cheyenne?"

"I'm going out to visit an old friend. She married a Westerner, you see. Polly's father ran a stagecoach stop, and she wed one of their drivers."

"How romantic!"

Ava smiled. "Yes, it was, really. I admit I was a bit jealous when she wrote me. I envy her life now. I haven't seen her for four years, and she's got a husband and two babies."

"It will be quite a reunion for you," Mr. Logan said.

"She's my dearest childhood friend. I can't wait to see her again." Ava hoped she wasn't chattering too much, or revealing too much about herself. Time to turn the conversation. "And what about you, Mr. Logan? I believe the conductor said you are going to San Francisco?"

"That's right. It's business. I shan't stay there more than a day or two, then it's back to Hartford."

They talked quite freely through the afternoon and shared their pleasure at the scenery their window afforded, which was new to both of them. As they rolled across the state of Missouri and headed northward for St. Joseph and the Nebraska border, Ava was grateful for congenial company. Mr. Logan's conversation was far from boring. He told her a bit about his sporadic work for a firm of lawyers in Hartford, and his hopes for steady employment if he succeeded in his mission to California. What that errand was, he did not divulge, but he certainly held her interest. The personable and handsome—yes, by now she admitted inwardly that he was very good looking—young man was an unexpected dividend for this trip.

After tomorrow, Mr. Logan would continue on his journey without her, while Ava began her visit with Polly and Jacob Tierney, but she was satisfied that her adventure had already begun. If nothing else out of the ordinary happened during her excursion, these hours spent in conversation with Mr. Logan were worth the time and expense of the trip.

"Oh, look! The moon is rising." Miss Neal leaned eagerly toward the window then sat back again. "I'm sorry, I'm blocking your view. Can you see it?"

"I can." Joe leaned forward to get a better look, being careful not to get too close to her. Their train was running northward for a ways, and so they looked out toward the east, where their view of the sky was unobstructed for several miles.

"Isn't it lovely?" she asked, so close that her breath

tickled his ear. "It's full tonight, isn't it?"

"Yes." He relaxed against the seat and studied her expression. His fingers itched for his drawing pencil, not to sketch the moon, but to capture her eager innocence.

"It looks huge, just on the horizon like that." She peered out again at the big, yellowish orb that hung like a glowing lantern over the hills in the distance.

"There'll be two full moons this month," Joe said. "A blue moon, they say, on the thirty-first."

"I hadn't realized. That's rare, isn't it?" She chuckled. "Of course. That's why they have the saying."

He nodded. "Once in a blue moon. I don't suppose it comes even once a year, but I'm not certain. Perhaps an almanac would tell."

"I'll have to look it up sometime."

"Next stop, St. Joe," the conductor called, coming down the aisle with a swinging gait. "Thirty minutes on the platform."

"Thirty minutes," Joe said. "That's hardly time for dinner, and we don't have a dining room on this train."

Ava hesitated. "Please don't think me forward, but I have some sandwiches that I bought in St. Louis. If you'd like, we could share them."

Joe grinned. "That sounds marvelous. Perhaps I can step off and get us some sarsaparilla or lemonade on the platform."

As soon as they stopped, he retrieved his hat and

stepped out into the sultry evening air. Dusk had fallen, and the moon was higher now and more normal looking, but still gorgeous in its plump roundness. What a beautiful evening—and his dinner companion would be a very charming young lady. He liked Miss Neal very much, especially her confidence. She didn't exhibit the timidity most women would if traveling alone, and she was making this solitary trip because she wanted to. She had made no apologies for her lack of a chaperone.

The memory of her auburn hair and glittering green eyes in the moonlight that shone through the window was firmly fixed in Joe's mind. He would definitely draw her portrait when they had parted company. A few minutes later, he made good on his word, returning to the car with not only bottled sarsaparilla but two apples and a half-dozen raisin cookies wrapped in brown paper.

Miss Neal surveyed the bounty. "Oh my, we're having a feast."

"Only the best for you, madam." Joe kept a straight face as he shook out his clean handkerchief and spread it on the seat between them. He put the apples and cookies on it, and Miss Neal added her sandwiches, which looked to be good, hearty sliced beef and cheese.

The two gentlemen who had sat opposite had both left the train. Joe sat down and eyed Miss Neal across the picnic supper. "Shall we ask the blessing?"

She seemed to accept that as normal and bowed her

head without signs of embarrassment, which was a relief to Joe.

"Dear Lord, we thank You for this and all Your gifts to us, and we ask Your care over the travelers on this train. Amen."

"Amen," Miss Neal said and reached for half a sandwich with a smile. "Thank you, Mr. Logan. This is so much nicer than bustling about the platform trying to find a bite."

"It is indeed."

They had fifteen minutes of comparative privacy, of which Joe made the most, plying his charming companion with questions about her life back home. He learned that her younger sister had been married only the week before.

"Conrad is a nice young man, and I'm sure they'll be happy," she said. "He has a position as headmaster at a secondary school, which is a recent advance from just plain schoolmaster. I'm sure that is why he was emboldened to speak to Sarah."

"Well, yes," Joe said, thinking of his own spotty income. "A man would have to be sure he was able to provide for his bride."

"Exactly. Last winter, when he was just a poor teacher, Sarah despaired of them ever being able to set up a household. This new opportunity for Conrad was a great blessing for them."

Joe nodded, watching Miss Neal's expressive green eyes. How long would it take for him to be able to present himself to some young lady's exacting father as an eligible suitor for the daughter? He hadn't been too troubled by the question until now, but the longer he conversed with Miss Neal, and the more he drank in her understated beauty and sweet features, the more he felt worthiness to be a desirable quality.

His mission on behalf of Mr. Becker's client grew in importance. If he had a regular job with the law firm in Hartford, he could begin to think about the possibility of courting a respectable young woman. Someone, if he were lucky, like Ava Neal. It wasn't just the full moon or the romance of meeting someone attractive on a journey to a strange place. Joe saw beyond that to the substance that lay beneath her captivating appearance.

These pleasant thoughts still flitted about Joe's mind in the morning, when the sleeper berths were folded away. He located Miss Neal during the first stop and once again took a seat beside her. He bought coffee and biscuits for both of them from a vendor who came through the train.

"Did you sleep well?" he asked her.

"Well enough. I don't suppose anyone sleeps quite perfectly on a train, and knowing I'll see Polly and her family today kept me a little on edge."

"Excited to see your friend?"

"Oh, yes!"

Joe nodded. Watching her face was a treat, but he would soon be denied this pleasure. "We're less than a hundred miles from Cheyenne."

"I'm all aflutter." She crumpled the paper that had wrapped her biscuit. "I suppose it's not for another three hours or so, but I'm already nervous."

Joe consulted his watch. "More like four. We have a couple more stops to make along the way."

Miss Neal glanced out the window. "We seem to be in quite desolate country now. Are there towns out here?"

"Not very big ones, I don't think. Cheyenne and Fort Laramie would be the largest in Wyoming, I'm guessing."

They ate their meager breakfast and continued to talk. It seemed fewer passengers boarded than left the train now. Joe and his companion marveled at the treeless expanse of plains they were crossing, but they also began to see hills, some of them thrusting up from the ground in unexpected places.

"If we could see out the front, perhaps we'd see mountains." Joe pushed himself up a little so he could better see forward. His finger slid into a break on the edge of the seat's upholstery. He smoothed the fabric down quickly, but he couldn't see anything from the windows ahead of them.

Miss Neal gave him a rueful smile. "I regret I won't be going far enough to see the Rocky Mountains. Maybe someday."

"This friend of yours," Joe said. "Surely her husband can't be driving a stagecoach now—not since they've taken the railway through?"

"He owns a short line of his own now, Polly tells me, from Cheyenne to a few smaller towns off the rail lines."

"I see."

The conductor came through, checking new passengers' tickets.

"Excuse me," Joe asked when he came even with their seats. "What's the next stop?"

"Pine Bluffs, but there's not much there. No restaurants or anything. There's a shack where the wagon trains used to trade a bit, and a few tents. One's a saloon. I expect it will draw more people now, since we stop there regular. There's some new stock pens, and a couple of ranchers put some cattle on the train this spring. Probably in the fall, we'll get more. Have to start hauling more cattle cars." He nodded at Ava. "Not far to Cheyenne after that, miss."

"Oh, thank you." Ava had foregone wearing her hat that morning, and she looked charming, but as soon as the conductor ambled on down the aisle, she began rummaging in her handbag. "I'm sorry, Mr. Logan, but I must find my gloves and put my hat on before we reach Cheyenne. Perhaps I can step into the lavatory while we're at Pine Bluffs and use the mirror in there."

"I'm sure you can. I'll get your hat down for you when we stop."

This preparation for leaving him unsettled Joe, as if she had cut the painter on a rowboat and would let him drift away. He took a deep breath. "Miss Neal, I shall miss your company on the rest of my trip."

Her fluttering hands stilled now that a plan for tending to her appearance was in place. "It's been good having someone congenial to talk to. I shall miss you, too."

Joe took courage. "Thank you. I wondered if you might consent to. . .to allowing me to write to you. I believe you said you'll be staying with your friend for several weeks?"

"We've planned on a month's stay." Her cheeks flushed a becoming pink. "I don't suppose it would be improper to receive a postal card from a fellow traveler."

"Thank you so much. You'll have to give me the address. It seems odd that I shall be back in New England before you, even though I'm journeying farther."

"Doesn't it?" She sobered. "I don't suppose we shall meet again after today, but yes, I'd like to stay in touch."

"I can—" Joe broke off as the train began to brake much more abruptly than when easing in at a station platform, throwing them both forward so hard he nearly fell. Instinctively, he put out an arm to break Miss Neal's flight. Even so, she plummeted to the floor between the facing pair of seats.

The train skidded to a halt with much squealing and grinding of metal on metal.

Joe braced himself until they stopped completely. He reached out to her. "Are you all right?"

"I think so." She brushed at her skirt and allowed him

to help her up onto the seat. "Why have we stopped so suddenly?"

"I don't know." Joe looked around the car. Other passengers were righting themselves and taking stock of their bruises and wayward possessions.

Miss Neal peered out the window. "I can't see anything on this side."

"Perhaps I can—" Joe started to rise but sank back into his seat as two men entered the front of the car with pistols in their hands.

Chapter 3

A woman on the other side of the aisle gave a little shriek.

"Easy now, folks," the closer gunman said. A grimy bandanna covered the lower part of his face, and his felt hat was pulled low on his brow. "Everybody stay calm and keep your hands where I can see 'em."

Ava tried to breathe, but she couldn't get enough air. All around her, the passengers gaped at the two men. Many of the travelers' faces had blanched, and the woman across the aisle clung to her companion's arm as though she would swoon at any second.

Ava glanced at Joe Logan. Like most of the other passengers, he held his hands at shoulder height and stared at the two robbers.

"If any of you have weapons, don't even think about using them," the robber said. "I guarantee I'm faster'n you, and keep in mind there's a lot of innocent bystanders in this car."

The second masked man stepped past his partner, holding out a gunny sack. "You can put the goods in this." He holstered his sidearm, but the first man continued to point his weapon at the passengers, sweeping the barrel slowly from side to side and letting his gaze focus on one after another.

The man with the sack stopped in front of the two men in the first seats. "All right, gents, let's have it. Wallets, watches, and anything else that might come in useful to me and my pals. If you've got pistols, knives, or derringers, might as well toss them in, too."

The two men scowled and began emptying their pockets.

Ava put a hand to her throat. *Polly's grandmother's brooch.* Could she possibly hide it before the robbers got this far down the aisle? It wasn't worth much, but she was determined to deliver it to Polly. Oh, why hadn't she left it in her bag? She had been foolish to think it would be safer pinned to her dress.

She fumbled with it. If she could undo the clasp and slide the pin free of fabric before the robbers noticed, she might have a chance of keeping it. Mr. Logan looked her way, and she froze. His gaze traveled to her hand then back to her eyes. Cautiously, he lowered one hand while watching the robbers and held it toward her.

Ava's heart thrummed as she slipped the cameo brooch off her bodice and slowly lowered her hand.

The vestibule door thudded open, and a third outlaw entered the car. Ava could barely hear the words he spoke to his companions.

"We got the engineer and fireman trussed up. Hurry up, though."

So there were more of them. While everyone else was distracted by the third robber's entrance, she slid the brooch into Mr. Logan's warm hand. His fingers closed over it. What would he do with it? He was closer to the aisle than she was.

As the robbers collected loot across the aisle, Mr. Logan bent his knees and stooped. He stuffed the brooch into an opening in the seam of the seat's upholstery and slowly straightened again, raising his hand to his former position.

"You!" The robbers faced them, one with his pistol pointed in Logan's face while the other held the open sack before him. "Let's have it. Wallet, watch, and anything else you've got."

Logan obediently reached inside his coat and pulled out his wallet. He hesitated, and the gunman waved the barrel at him.

"Drop it in, mister! Now!"

Logan let it fall into the sack.

"Empty your pockets," the man holding the sack snarled.

Logan pulled out a watch on a chain, a pocketknife, and a few coins and dropped them in the sack.

"That all?"

Mr. Logan nodded.

"What's that?" The gunman nodded toward the leather valise beneath the seat.

"Just, uh, papers and such," Mr. Logan said.

"Open it."

With a resigned expression, he bent and retrieved the case and unbuckled it. The robber with the sack peered inside. "What have we here?" He took out a small parcel wrapped in brown paper.

"It's nothing," Mr. Logan said.

"Hmm."

"Step lively, Bert," the robber's companion growled.

Bert dropped the package into his sack and looked at Ava.

"Now you, lady."

Ava's heart lurched. She opened her handbag and took out her small leather change purse. She stared into the gunman's steely gray eyes as she held it over the sack and let go.

"You got any more?"

"No, sir."

"Maybe better put the whole thing in there," he said, eyeing her handbag.

"Oh, must I? There's nothing else of value to you."

A lump ached in Ava's throat. Her purse wouldn't matter that much—it now held only her comb, a few hairpins, a small container of pomade, and a fan. But why should these thugs take it?

"Come on, we ain't got all day." The man holding the gun seemed rather impatient. Bert grunted and moved on to the next set of seats. Ava looked sidelong at Mr. Logan. His gaze followed the gunnysack, and his mouth was set in a grim line.

As soon as the robbers had left the car, Joe raced to the front door. The train rested in the middle of nowhere, with uneven plains stretching away for miles around them. He heard a commotion of hoofbeats, and a moment later a band of six horsemen appeared ahead of the locomotive, galloping off and veering away from the rail lines toward the southwest.

The conductor appeared at the main door of the car ahead. Joe waved to him. "Anyone hurt?"

The conductor hopped down and walked toward him. Satisfied he wouldn't do that if the train were about to move, Joe climbed down the steps and met him halfway.

"Apparently two of their men boarded the train at the last stop," the conductor said. "Their friends laid a pile of rocks and brush on the tracks and forced us to stop. We'll have to clear it."

Joe looked around. "They must have hauled it a long way."

"There's hills and ravines on the other side. They probably came out here and got it ready long in advance."

"I thought there were railroad police traveling on the trains now," Joe said.

"We've got one. He was in the next car, but they spotted him first thing and got the drop on him as soon as we started braking. They roughed him up a little and tied him up. There wasn't a thing he could do."

"Is he all right?"

The conductor nodded. "Mostly. I imagine he'll be back soon to talk to the folks in your car. It'll be hard for them to identify the robbers, though, with their faces covered."

They walked together to the entrance of the car in which Joe had been riding. The conductor entered first and called out, "Everybody all right?"

"If you call losing a hundred and twenty dollars all right," a man replied.

"I'm sorry, sir, but as your ticket stated, the railroad is not responsible for losses in robberies. Unfortunately, the gangs are getting bolder and, it seems, a little smarter. We've got a detective up ahead in the next car. The robbers beat him up a little, but he's starting to talk to the people up there and get their stories. He'll be back here in a few minutes. Be ready to tell him what you lost and also any details you recall about the robbers. Once you've done that, gentlemen, we could use your help in clearing the tracks so we can get under way again as soon as possible."

Joe slid into the seat next to Miss Neal. "I hope you're not too shaken by this unfortunate incident."

"It could have been so much worse," she said. "Are you all right?"

"I'm fine, but. . ."

"They stole something from your valise," she said. "Was it important?"

"Yes."

"I'm sorry."

He gazed into her sympathetic eyes for a moment. "Thank you. I shall have to disembark at Cheyenne and send a telegram to my employer."

"Oh dear."

"Yes."

He felt along the edge of the seat and located the break in the seam. After a moment's probing, he retrieved her brooch and held it out to her.

"Oh, thank you!" Miss Neal took it and gazed at it. "I can't tell you how much this means to me. My friend Polly's grandmother asked me to take it to Polly, and I was afraid I would lose it to those bandits. I don't suppose it's worth much, but Polly will be so happy to get it." Her eyes flickered. "You lost your watch, too, and all your funds, I suppose."

He leaned toward her and lowered his voice. "Not so bad as all that. It was a cheap watch, and I've got twenty dollars hidden on my person, so I'll be all right."

Her face flushed, and she whispered, "I have a bit of cash sewn into a seam myself. My mother insisted, and she was wiser than I gave her credit for."

"Good." He picked up the valise from where he had let it fall after the robbers took his parcel. From it he took out a tablet and pencil. He flipped open to a blank white page and began to draw with swift, sure lines.

"Oh! You didn't tell me you are an artist," Miss Neal said.

"Of sorts." He glanced at her apologetically. "If you'll forgive me, this may be important."

"Of course."

She watched him sketch the face of the robber who had held the sack. Joe hadn't been able to see his entire face, but he had taken note of the shape of his nose, eyes, and brow, and the full growth of beard that showed on the sides, where the bandanna didn't cover it all.

The detective entered the car with a small notepad in hand. The lines at the corners of his mouth bespoke fatigue and maybe some embarrassment at his inability to stop the robbery. He went down the aisle fairly quickly, taking each passenger's list of stolen items and descriptions of the robbers. When he reached their seats, Joe nodded toward his companion.

"Miss Neal."

While she told the detective about the change purse and small amount of cash she had lost, Joe put the finishing touches on his second drawing. This one wasn't as good—he hadn't managed to catch as many details of the gunman's face. He didn't even attempt to draw the third man. He had concentrated instead on memorizing enough to make an accurate drawing of one man and a passable likeness of the second.

"What's this?" The detective leaned over him.

"That's one of the robbers, sir." Joe flipped back to the previous page. "This is the one who held the bag of loot. His companion called him Bert. If you'd like to come back here after you've spoken to the others, I can also draw the gunman's pistol for you."

"That one looks just like the man with the sack," Miss Neal said, pointing to the drawing of Bert.

"Hmm, these could be helpful," the detective said. "What's your name, sir?"

"Joseph Logan. I lost some very valuable property, which I was employed to deliver to San Francisco, as well as my wallet and my watch."

Joe went to join the other men who were clearing the tracks, and soon the train was once more moving toward Cheyenne. He kept up a conversation with the charming Miss Neal, but his mind kept going over the robbery. If he had put the parcel in his coat pocket, the robbers might not have gotten it. . .or perhaps if he'd stuffed it inside his hat on the overhead rack. Ah, well. Too late to change anything now.

When they pulled in at the station, Miss Neal gazed out the window anxiously and seized his wrist when the train was nearly halted.

"There's Polly, and that must be Jacob with her! They've brought the children. Oh, I'm so thrilled to be here."

Joe wished he had time now to draw her portrait, with her features so animated. Maybe later—he knew he wouldn't forget her soon.

"I hope you have a wonderful visit with them."

"Thank you. And again, thank you so much for your help during the robbery. I wish it had turned out better for you."

"I'll be all right." He said the words blithely, but his heart was heavy. Mr. Becker would certainly not be pleased with his performance.

"Will you come and meet them?"

He almost declined, citing the need to get his telegram off quickly. But what difference would a few minutes make? He would not be taking the train on to San Francisco, he was sure.

He gave Miss Neal his hand down the steps, and Polly Tierney dashed up and swept her friend into her arms.

"Ava! Your train was so late, and we heard the station master say something about a holdup. What happened?"

"It's true," Miss Neal said, smiling as though the whole thing had been a picnic. "We were robbed. But we're fine."

"Oh dear! You'll have to tell us the whole story later." Mrs. Tierney pulled her husband forward. He was cradling the baby in one arm and held a two-year-old's hand firmly with the other. "This is Jacob, and Harry Clyde, and the baby is Amelia."

"How lovely! And I'd like you all to meet Mr. Logan, who was of greatest assistance on the journey since St. Louis, especially during the robbery."

Joe greeted them all and turned down an invitation to join them for supper.

"I'm sorry. It sounds delightful, but I need to send a wire to my employer right away and get his instructions."

"Well, thank you for looking after Ava," Polly said, appraising him with her china-blue eyes. "If you're in town any length of time, please call on us."

"Thank you, ma'am." Joe shook hands with Jacob Tierney and turned to Miss Neal. "It's been delightful. I hope we meet again."

She held out her gloved hand. As Joe took it and studied her sweet face, he realized how much he meant those words. But the next moment, Miss Neal took the baby in her arms and Polly led her friend and young Harry Clyde toward the family's wagon, while Jacob went in search of their guest's luggage.

Joe turned away, squared his shoulders, and asked for

directions to the telegraph office.

He kicked around town while waiting for a reply to his brief message.

TRAIN ROBBED PACKET AND PAPERS LOST SEND INSTRUCTIONS

There seemed no need to go into detail. Becker and Fixx would see that the telegram came from Cheyenne and would decide what they wanted him to do. The stationmaster informed him that the next eastbound train wouldn't go through until the next morning, so Joe set out walking, suitcase in hand.

The city was young and raw, but full-blown in its offering of commerce. Cattle pens spread out beyond the railroad depot. Hundreds of businesses lined the streets, from small shacks with signs declaring them to be gun shops, saddle makers, or grocers, to substantially built hotels and emporiums. Joe hadn't expected to see a sturdy hardware store flanked by a barbershop and a lawyer's office. There seemed any number of places where a man could risk his money in a card game or buy a glass of beer. He found a restaurant that offered fresh beefsteak and rhubarb pie. Suddenly ravenous, he entered and sat down on one side of a long table where a dozen men were already eating.

The tasty meal fortified him, but Joe was still uneasy and knew he would be until he heard from Mr. Becker.

He asked the restaurant's owner for the name of a quiet hotel. After he'd registered, he checked the view from his second-floor window and decided that if this was a quiet hotel, the ones nearer the railroad and stockyards must be noisy indeed. He could count four saloon signs without leaning out the window. The desk clerk had mentioned that Cheyenne was known as "the gambling capital of the world." Joe decided to stay in that evening. He couldn't chance losing the small amount of money he had left.

But first he must check to see if his employer had replied to his telegram. He wandered back to the train station by a different path and discovered more saloons, dance halls, and gambling dens, as well as a trader who bought buffalo hides and a group of Indian women sitting beneath a canvas roof not far from the depot, selling moccasins, baskets, and other handmade items.

His telegram came in just minutes before the office was scheduled to close for the night. Joe stared down at the words, his stomach churning.

HALF PAY ON RETURN EMPLOYMENT TERMINATED

He shoved the slip of paper into his pocket and trudged toward his hotel.

Chapter 4

The next day, Ava slept late and then joined Polly in the kitchen of the snug little frame house on the outskirts of Cheyenne. She ate a hearty breakfast and then held the baby while Polly coaxed young Harry Clyde to finish his oatmeal.

"Jacob's taking a stage to Horse Creek," Polly said. "He won't be back until this evening. Would you like to go shopping or just rest today?"

"Let's take it easy, unless you need something in town," Ava said. "I'd like to get used to not jostling along and have a chance to get acquainted with your adorable children."

Polly got up and went to the stove for the coffeepot. "All right. You must tell me all the news from home, and

131

every detail about the wedding."

"It was lovely," Polly replied. "Sarah was the most beautiful bride I've ever seen. And they've gone to New York for their honeymoon. Conrad promised to show her all the sights."

Polly sighed. "New York. I'm sure she'll enjoy it, but I'm afraid I would feel claustrophobic now. Cheyenne is bad enough. Those years I spent on the prairie with Ma and Pa at the stagecoach stop, I learned to appreciate the open land."

"Where are your parents now?" Ava asked.

Polly laughed. "Three streets over. Pa's got a position with the railroad. He weighs the freight and makes out the invoices."

"Sounds like good, steady work."

"It is, and I think Pa likes not having to worry about the stock and the Indians and all of that."

Ava frowned. "You told me you never had any trouble with the Indians."

"We didn't, where we were. Some of the stations were attacked, but on Pa's section of the line, we had more trouble with robbers." She chuckled. "Now they've moved on to train holdups."

"Yes." Ava pushed aside the memory of the robbery. "It will be good to see your folks again."

"We'll take the kids over to see Ma tomorrow, if you like. Though it wouldn't surprise me if Ma showed up here today to check on you. She's as anxious to see a face from home as I was."

"Oh, that reminds me. I have some things from your grandmother." Ava stood and handed Amelia to Polly. "Here, take her for a minute, and I'll go fetch them."

A moment later she was back in the kitchen with the two books and jar of chokecherry jelly Grandma Winfield had pressed her to carry to Polly. Harry Clyde had been excused and was now playing on the floor with a half-grown puppy they called Spot.

"Here are your goodies." Ava laid the gifts on the table.

"Oh, how sweet of her." Polly picked up the jar of clear red preserves. "She knows I've always loved her jelly, and I can't find the chokecherries out here." She opened the covers of the books. "Dickens and poetry. I shall have to write Grandma a nice long letter. There's talk of starting a public library in town, but I can never lay hands on enough books to suit me."

"There's more." Ava sat down across from her and held out her closed hand. She opened it, revealing the cameo brooch in her palm.

Polly gasped. "Grandma sent me her cameo?"

"Yes. She told me she had especially wanted you to have it, but she didn't dare send it by post. I guess she was wise in that, though I nearly lost it in the train robbery."

"So, they didn't look in the baggage?" Polly asked.

"It wasn't in the baggage. I was actually wearing it, to

make sure it wouldn't get lost."

Polly gazed at her with wide eyes. "Did they not think it was valuable then? Grandma always told me this was her most precious piece of jewelry, though I don't suppose it's worth an awful lot."

Ava felt the heat rise in her cheeks, all the way to her hairline. "Do you remember the young man I introduced you to on the platform? Joe Logan?"

"Oh, sure." Polly eyed her carefully. "What about him?"

"You only have that brooch now thanks to Mr. Logan."

"Really?"

"Mm-hmm." Ava plunked down in the chair where she had sat for breakfast. There was no getting out of telling the whole tale now. "He rescued it from the robbers. Otherwise I'd have had to toss it in their vile gunnysack." She shuddered. "I felt so bad about it. I mean, he lost his watch and his wallet, and even the things his employer had given him to deliver."

"That's a shame." Polly shifted the baby to her other shoulder. "What's he going to do?"

"I don't know. I think he was afraid he would lose his job over it. But even in the middle of that, he helped me save your grandma's brooch. And afterward, he drew pictures of the robbers for the police." She smiled wanly at Polly. "He's quite an artist."

"I see he made quite an impression on you."

"Well. . ." Ava laughed and waved a hand through the

air. "He was nice, and I admit I enjoyed his company, but I'll probably never see him again."

"I'll try to take your mind off that," Polly said.

"By showing me the West?"

"Yes, but besides that, Jacob and I have several unmarried friends."

Ava shook her head. "I came out here to visit you, dear, not to marry a stagecoach driver as you did."

"We haven't got so many drivers now, and the best of those are married, but I'm serious. There's a fellow at the feed store you might find interesting. I'm sure he'd be interested in you."

"Oh, really, I don't—"

"Then there are the Crawford brothers. They have a ranch west of here. They're a little shy, but they're good men, both of them, and they go to our church. We could invite them over for dinner on Sunday."

"Please don't. I'd feel like merchandise on display."

"Well, it's no secret there's a shortage of decent, eligible women out here. And you can't avoid meeting several bachelors at the Independence Day celebration tomorrow."

"Tomorrow? You're right—tomorrow's the Fourth. I fear I'd lost track on my trip."

"There are going to be speeches and displays and races and a shooting match, all over near the stockyards. There's a big field where they hold livestock auctions, with benches and—"

The puppy yipped in the next room, and a clang sounded, followed by a thud. Polly jumped up, holding Amelia out to Ava.

"Harry Clyde, what was that?"

"Nothin'."

"It's never nothing." Polly hurried into the small parlor, and Ava followed. In the middle of the modestly furnished room, Harry Clyde wriggled on the floor, with Spot licking his face. One of the toddler's shoes lay a couple feet away, beside the fireplace poker. Polly sighed and stooped to pick it up. "At least there's no fire today. Come on, young man. Let's get your shoe back on. I think it's time we took Spot outside and showed Aunt Ava the garden."

"And the chickens?" Harry's eyes lit with excitement.

"Yes, and the chickens."

Ava sat down on the rug beside them. She would rather concentrate on Polly and her family, especially since Joe Logan had no doubt left Cheyenne already. "Will you show them to me, Harry Clyde?" she said. "I adore chickens."

Joe packed his few belongings in his suitcase and picked up the leather valise that had held the package. Heading home in defeat did not sit well with him. The one bright spot on this entire journey was Ava Neal, and now he would board a train taking him away from her.

He ate breakfast in the hotel dining room and walked slowly to the depot, but he was still an hour early for the train. A few yards from the ticket window was the railroad police's cubbyhole of an office, and on a whim, he stopped in.

The man behind the desk wore a suit as nice as those the lawyers wore back in Connecticut. Joe pulled his hat off and nodded.

"Good morning. I'm Joseph Logan. I was on the train yesterday when it was robbed. I wondered if there had been any progress in catching the thieves."

The man jumped up and came around the desk. "I'm Dan Colson. So you're the fellow who drew the sketches."

Joe nodded with a tight smile.

"As a matter of fact, there has been some progress," Colson said. "The local sheriff recognized the bagman from your drawing as Ed Robbins. They'd had him up before, for theft and disorderly conduct. They nabbed him late last night at his own house. He's not talking, though, and we haven't caught the rest of them yet."

"Well, that's something," Joe said.

"Yes. And they've recovered some money and things from Robbins that they're sure came off the train—including four pocket watches. I don't suppose you lost your watch to them?"

"Yes, I did. But I'd much rather hear they've found the packet I was carrying for my employer."

"Hmm. Don't know about that, but Detective Simms might be able to tell you."

"Him being the one who was on the train yesterday?" Joe asked.

"One and the same."

"Where could I find him?"

"He's set to travel on the eastbound today, and he'll probably stop in here in—oh, twenty minutes or so." The man glanced at the clock hanging on the wall near the door. "You can wait for him if you'd like. They've got the recovered valuables in the vault over at the bank, until they can sort out what belongs to whom. If there's time, Simms might let you take a look for your package."

With renewed hope, Joe took a seat on a bench just outside the office and waited for Detective Simms.

A few minutes later, Simms came around, wearing a suit and bowler hat and carrying a small leather bag. He spotted Joe and stopped on the boardwalk. "Hello, Logan. Heading east today?"

"Yes. That is, unless you've recovered my parcel."

"Hmm, I don't recall anything like what you described yesterday, but we can go over to the bank and take a look if you wish." Simms pulled out his watch and opened it. "There's time if we don't dawdle." He poked his head into Colson's office. "Dan, I'm taking Mr. Logan round to the bank. I'll be back."

"Right," Colson said.

The banker obliged them by bringing out the box of items the lawmen had recovered from Ed Robbins's house, minus the cash.

"The railroad's orders are to return cash claimed on a prorated basis. You'll have to file a claim for that at the office."

"I did that, thanks." Joe poked through the box. "I don't see my wallet, or the parcel."

"How about those watches? Is one of them yours?"

Simms and Joe pulled four pocket watches from the hoard, but none of them was right. All were of distinctive designs, and three bore engraved names or initials.

"Those are all better than the cheap one I was carrying." Joe placed the last one back in Simms's hand.

"Well, they may have emptied all the wallets and purses into a general fund and then divided it," Simms said. "I didn't see your Miss Neal's coin purse, either. Do you know if she filed a form for the cash she lost?"

"Yes, I'm sure she did."

"What was in this parcel you're so keen on?" Simms asked.

Joe huffed out a breath. "It's a little embarrassing, but I don't know, exactly."

"How's that?"

"I was delivering it for an attorney. He didn't tell me what it was, but it was some sort of inheritance for the recipient—a woman. I had the idea it was jewelry."

"There's a few pieces in there, but we know this isn't nearly all of the loot." Simms fished a bracelet and several rings from the box.

Joe shook his head. "I wish I knew for sure what I was carrying. I was just the messenger, you see."

"Might be worth stopping over a day and asking the lawyer to wire a description. And who knows? The marshal might catch the rest of the gang and get back some more of the stuff."

"That's a thought," Joe said. Either way, it wouldn't hurt him to spend another day in Cheyenne, and he admitted to himself that the possibility of looking up Ava and her friends appealed strongly to him. "I'll do it."

Simms nodded and signaled to the banker that they were finished with the box. "As for me, I've got to get on the train in a few minutes. We'll be more vigilant than ever since this latest holdup. There'll be two of us on the outgoing train, in addition to the express agent in the express car—though I don't expect the robbers to hit us again so soon."

"They might," Joe said. "If they're smart, they'll hit you when you least expect it."

"True." Simms smiled grimly as they stepped out onto the sidewalk. "Dan Colson, over at the railroad office, was impressed by your drawings. They were instrumental in identifying Robbins, you know."

"I'm glad."

"They'll probably place them in evidence for when he goes to trial." As they talked, they walked toward the train station. Colson's door was open, and when they reached it, Simms paused and looked in.

"I'll be boarding as soon as the train pulls in, Dan."

Mr. Colson looked up from his desk. "All right. Logan, did you find what you were looking for?"

"No, sir, but Simms suggested I wire the sender and ask for a description of the contents of his parcel, in case the outlaws opened the parcel and dumped it in with the rest of the stuff."

"Good idea." Colson rose and came to the doorway. "Say, Logan, you've got a good eye. We can use observant men like you. Not looking for work, are you?"

"With the railroad?"

"Sure. The pay's good, and the work's steady. Right, Simms?"

The detective chuckled. "Oh, it's steady, all right. There's the train. See you later, Dan." He strode off toward the ticket window as a locomotive's whistle cut the air.

Joe watched him walk away and turned to face Mr. Colson. "I'm interested, sir."

Colson nodded. "Terrific. Have you ever been arrested, son?"

"No, sir."

"Good. I suppose you were too young to serve during the war."

"I joined up the last year, as soon as I turned eighteen. First Connecticut Infantry."

"Can you give me a couple of references for general character?"

Joe did some quick thinking. He wouldn't dare put down Mr. Becker after his recent failure for Becker and Fixx, but there was a Hartford accountant he had done several small jobs for, and he was in good standing with his landlady. He could approximate an address for his old sergeant, too. "Yes, I can."

"Better and better. You go send your wire and come back here. We'll talk. If things work out, maybe I can send you on the westbound first thing in the morning, with one of our detectives. You'd be gone overnight. It would let you get a feel for the job. What do you say? One of our most experienced men will be on that train."

"It sounds good."

Colson handed him a pencil and a sheet of paper. "Write down your references, so I can send a couple of wires. What town did you say you're from?"

"Hartford, Connecticut, sir."

"Right. I'll contact their police department, too. Standard part of the hiring process." He watched Joe keenly.

"I wouldn't expect any less, sir."

Colson smiled. "Good. Now, do you have a sidearm?"

"No, sir."

"Hmm, I'll ask Detective Allen if he can lend you one."

Colson took the paper on which Joe had written the names of the people he thought would vouch for him. "Come back here in a couple of hours, and maybe we can talk some more."

Joe headed for the telegraph office feeling better about his prospects than he had in a long time. And to be able to stay out here in the West—he'd never expected anything like this to happen. He was sorry he'd lost Becker's package, but maybe some good would come of it.

And there was Miss Neal. He didn't dare hope the railroad would allow him to stay in Cheyenne long, but there was always a chance he would meet up with her again.

Chapter 5

Ava tried not to stare, but wherever she turned some colorful new sight met her gaze. Men were leading sleek horses to the stock pens while soldiers set up targets for the shooting contest. Vendors called out to the passersby in hopes of selling everything from glasses of switchel to firecrackers.

"Not like back home, is it?" Polly asked with a laugh.

"No, not at all." Back in Massachusetts, Independence Day was celebrated with enthusiasm, too, but it had a certain serenity and dignity about it. Ladies strolled about on the arms of their beaux or husbands, showing off their summer bonnets and sipping lemonade. The speeches were applauded calmly, and the fireworks were saved for evening. Boys who broke that rule by setting off firecrackers and scaring the horses were reprimanded severely. Here, everyone seemed to expect a small explosion at least every minute, and the livestock didn't seem too upset by it.

Jacob, like most business owners except the saloon-keepers, had closed his office for the day. No freight runs on the Fourth of July. The entire town seemed to have put business aside and thronged the celebration area. Jacob carried the baby, while Polly and Ava took turns holding on to Harry Clyde's hand.

"There's the pastor," Jacob said, nodding to where several men stood talking.

"Let's introduce Ava." The warmth in Polly's voice made Ava suspicious.

Jacob was agreeable, and so they ambled toward the group.

"Well hello, Tierneys," called a man of about forty. He wore a conservative suit and a ribbon tie.

"Morning, Pastor." Jacob led them over. "This young lady is Polly's friend from Massachusetts, Miss Neal. She took the train out here to visit us. Ava, this is Pastor Worth."

"Welcome," the minister said, smiling at Ava. "That's quite a journey you undertook."

"It was interesting," Ava said. "I'm glad you have the railroad now. It really wasn't too arduous, compared to the trip Polly made when she first came out here with her parents."

The two men Pastor Worth had been conversing with were younger than he was, and both watched Ava with interest while she spoke.

"Allow me to introduce two of our church members," the pastor said, nodding toward them. "Hap Leland works at one of the local ranches, and Bill Ingram is employed at the mercantile on Central Avenue."

"How do you do, gentlemen?" Both returned her greeting heartily. Ava felt her face flush. Was this the reason for Polly's eagerness to show her around?

"Glad you had a safe journey, ma'am." Bill ducked his head and glanced at her then swiftly away.

"Well, it's not like she wasn't on the train when that outlaw gang held it up," Jacob said.

"You wasn't!" Hap's eyebrows rose.

Bill muttered, "Good gracious."

"I see you came through the ordeal unscathed," the pastor said.

"Yes. No one was hurt so far as I know," Ava said. "We passengers are all a little lighter in our purses, I'm afraid."

Jacob shifted little Amelia to his other arm. "I heard last night they'd caught one of the robbers."

"Perhaps some of the stolen goods will be recovered," the pastor said.

"I got held up once," Hap put in. "Was on the stage from Salt Lake. You ever get held up, Jacob?"

"Once or twice, a few years back, when I was working for the Overland," Jacob said. "But that's not a very pleasant topic for the ladies. What's on the agenda for today?"

"Governor Campbell will speak at noon, over at the Methodist Church," Pastor Worth said.

Ava glanced at Polly. "How exciting! Will we get to meet the governor?"

"I expect so," Polly said. "He's generally quite sociable at events like this."

"My father will be so impressed." Ava smiled at the minister. "You see, he told my mother this trip would be educational for me—and he was right, in so many ways."

"Did you tell 'em about the train robbery?" Bill asked.

Jacob glared at him, but Ava didn't mind the question.

"It's all right, Jacob. And the answer is, not yet. I wrote them a nice long letter yesterday, telling them I'd arrived safely and all about Polly and her family and their home, but I left out a few things, you might say. I'll probably tell them when I go home. I don't really want to keep it from them, but I know my mother would worry about me if she heard it now, and I'm not close enough for her to prod all over and make sure I'm still in one piece."

All the adults laughed, but by this time Harry Clyde was getting quite fidgety and pulling against Polly's firm grip.

"We'd better take this little fellow to see the horses," Polly said.

"Horses," Harry Clyde shouted.

"All right, young man." Jacob looked at the others. "See you later."

"If any of you gentlemen wish to join us at noon, you're welcome," Polly said.

"Thank you," Pastor Worth replied. "My wife is about here somewhere. She packed us a lunch, but if she hasn't promised anyone else, we'll be happy to eat with you."

"I might catch up to you," Hap said.

"I told the boss I'd eat with him and the missus." Bill was clearly unhappy to make the pronouncement, his gaze resting on Ava.

"Well, it was nice meeting you," she said and walked away with Polly and Jacob.

"They're both nice young men," Polly assured her. "Especially Bill, but he's on the shy side."

"Hap's all right, too," Jacob added. "I suppose he'd seem a little wild if you set him down in Boston, but ranch life does that to a man."

"You two know I didn't come out here looking for a husband, don't you?" Ava asked sternly.

Jacob laughed. "Is that right? From what Polly's been saying these last few weeks, I had the opposite impression."

"Hush, you!" Polly glared at him and then chuckled. "I'm sorry, Ava. I'll try not to foist too many young men on you, especially not ones who aren't of the first water. But there is one fellow I want you to meet—"

"Not Neil Conyers," Jacob said.

Polly stopped walking. "Yes, Neil Conyers. What's wrong with him?" To Ava she said quickly, "He's a blacksmith."

"He's from Alabama."

"So?"

Jacob shrugged. "I don't know. I didn't suppose she'd want to attach herself to someone from the South."

Polly turned to Ava with eyebrows raised. "My dear, you recall the late unpleasantness between the North and South?"

"Uh. . .yes," Ava replied, not sure whether to laugh or not.

"Well, it makes no difference to me—or to Jacob"—she shot her husband a meaningful look—"where a man hails from. But if you don't fancy a southern accent. . ."

"Mr. Conyers can't be too prejudiced toward the South if he's voluntarily left it for Wyoming Territory," Ava said.

"My thinking exactly." Polly nodded in triumph.

Jacob raised his free hand in surrender. "Fine. And Neil is a nice fellow. But I can't always understand what he's saying, his accent's so thick."

"We'll let Ava be the judge of that." Polly took her friend's arm and began walking toward the stock pens. "If you see him, Jacob, be sure to invite him to eat with us."

"The way things are going, we'll have an army to feed

out of your lunch basket," Jacob said with a tolerant smile. "But then, you always pack enough to feed a regiment."

Ava said nothing, but in her mind, she knew none of the young men on Polly's list could quite match her standard. And what was that standard? To her surprise, it wasn't Will Sandford who came to mind, but a certain blue-eyed man she had met on the train from St. Louis.

Joe walked with Jacob Tierney down the board sidewalk until it ended and they stepped down to street level.

"I walk to the stage stop every day, because it's so close," Jacob said, "but I suppose it's a mile from your hotel."

"That's all right," Joe assured him. Two days had passed since he had been hired by the railroad, and much of the intervening time had been spent sitting in either a passenger car or an express car, which carried freight as well as safes for valuables.

"We'll have to make sure we don't keep you too late." Jacob gestured toward a small frame house set back from the street. "There it is, home sweet home."

"It looks comfortable."

"It is, though it wasn't much more than a shack when we first bought it. Polly's pa helped me fix it up."

Joe followed him around to the back stoop. His host didn't knock, but opened the door and entered the warm, lamp-lit kitchen.

"Hey, Polly, what's to eat?" he called.

Polly came to him, laughing. "I told Ava you'd say that."

"Papa!" Harry Clyde ran toward them and launched himself into Jacob's arms.

"Well, hello yourself, kid." Jacob tossed the little boy in the air and then set him down and gave Polly a quick kiss. He looked at Ava, who stood near the cookstove. "Ava." He stepped aside so the ladies could see his guest. "Look who I found at the station when I got back from Horse Creek. He was kicking his heels and looking hungry, so I dragged him on home for supper."

"We've got plenty." Polly wiped her hands on her apron and stepped forward. "Mr. Logan, isn't it?"

"Yes, ma'am. Good to see you again." Joe took her outstretched hand for a moment. "I hope it's no bother."

"Not a bit," Polly said.

Joe looked beyond her, and his gaze settled on Ava. She stood with a wooden spoon in her hand, a patchwork apron tied about her waist. Her auburn hair was pulled back with a green satin ribbon, and she stared at him but lowered her eyes when she caught his gaze. His pulse surged, and he realized he'd been anticipating this moment all day.

"Miss Neal," he managed to say smoothly.

"Mr. Logan, I'm so glad you came. We had no idea you were still in town. Or have you been to San Francisco and back already?" She set down the spoon and came toward him, her eyes bright.

"I've been partway there and back again. Changed my mind about heading east the other day."

"I've wondered how your business turned out," Ava said. "Perhaps you can tell us over supper."

"I'd be happy to."

Jacob showed him where he could wash up. When they had settled at the table a few minutes later, Joe enjoyed Polly and Ava's cooking.

"That's the best meat loaf I've had since I left Hartford," he said.

"Thank you," Polly said. "And Mr. Logan, I understand I owe you my thanks."

"What for?"

"Ava said that without your help, I wouldn't have received Grandma Winfield's brooch."

"Oh, that. I was happy I could do it and that we succeeded in thwarting the outlaws on a small scale. But won't you call me Joe? I wish you all would." His gaze lingered on Ava, and her cheeks seemed to go a shade pinker, but she was smiling.

"And you've no word on the items you lost?" she asked.

"Not yet, but my former employer did send a description of the articles in the parcel, so that I'll be able to identify them positively if they're found."

"What was it?" Polly put a hand to her mouth. "I'm sorry. I shouldn't ask."

"It's all right. Turns out it was jewelry, which I had suspected. Family pieces, worth a few hundred dollars, but of greater sentimental value to the one who would have received them."

"Like my brooch."

"Yes, sort of. But this was a pendant and a matching set of earrings. Garnets and marcasite."

"Oh, it sounds lovely," Polly said.

In the next room the baby cried, and Ava jumped up.

"Let Aunt Ava get her."

She brought Amelia to the table and held her on her lap while she continued to eat, even giving her tiny bites of mashed potato off her plate. Joe marveled at how Ava took to the children. She seemed to outright adore young Harry Clyde, but without telling the little lad as much.

When they had finished eating and lingered over more coffee, Joe revealed that he would be moving the next day from his hotel to a boardinghouse.

Jacob leaned back in his chair and said, "So, does that mean you're staying?"

Joe smiled. "I am. I've been hired by the railroad police."

Ava gasped. "Your drawings. I knew they would be impressed."

"Yes, that was what led to the offer. I'll need some training, though. For the next couple of weeks I'll be learning about firearms and studying maps and how safes are constructed—and demolished. Things like that."

"That's marvelous," Ava said. "I know you were uncertain about your other job."

"Yes. They fired me, first thing when they heard I'd lost the package. Two words on a telegram—it cost them sixty cents to tell me." Joe shook his head. "Ah, well, the Lord knew, didn't He?"

"That's right," Ava said. "Some good has come out of this."

Polly chuckled. "Next thing, you'll be saying you're glad you were robbed."

"I won't go that far."

Polly turned to Joe. "Do put cotton wool in your ears if you're going to be doing a lot of shooting practice. Bob Dexter, the gunsmith, is deaf as a post from test-firing all those guns he fixes."

"I'll keep that in mind," Joe said, but he was watching Ava. He hesitated to produce his gift but decided to go ahead. "Speaking of the robbery, though, reminds me of something I brought you." He reached inside his jacket pocket and brought out a sheet of paper from his sketchbook and unfolded it. He passed it to Ava, observing her face anxiously.

"Why—it's me!" She smiled and held the drawing out to her friend. "See, Polly? I'm wearing your cameo, just as I did on the train."

"It's not a very good likeness," Joe said. "I can see that, now that I have you right here before me. But I was drawing from memory, and—"

"It's excellent," Polly declared, glancing from Ava to the drawing and back again.

"Next time, I shall do better." *Tonight when I get to my room.* He hadn't caught the shimmer of her glossy hair, or the exact tilt of her chin. But the next portrait would capture both.

"I'm immensely flattered," Ava said. "Am I meant to keep this?"

"If you like."

"I do. Very much."

At the end of an evening of pleasant conversation, Ava walked with him to the door. Joe didn't hesitate to put in a request.

"I wonder if I might call on you next week."

Her lashes swept down, shielding her green eyes for a moment.

"Why, yes. I'd like that. And I don't think Polly and Jacob would mind."

They settled on the details of the meeting, and Joe set out for his hotel, whistling as he walked.

Chapter 6

Jacob came through the back door two nights later and scooped Harry Clyde up into his arms. "They're saying in town that the marshal and the railroad detectives have gone out after the gang of train robbers," he told Polly and Ava.

"Not another robbery, I hope," Polly said, frowning.

"I don't think so. Maybe they got a tip on where to find them."

Polly sighed. "I hope they don't start robbing the stage-coaches."

"We don't carry the really valuable stuff anymore," Jacob said. "At least not often. But those outlaws were all my drivers could talk about today."

"Well, I hope they catch the men who hit the train I

came on," Ava said.

Polly nodded emphatically. "So do I."

Jacob carried Harry Clyde over to the rack near the back door. "Maybe Joe Logan can tell us more when he comes around on Saturday night."

Ava said nothing, but her heart felt torn. Every time she thought about Joe's impending call, she wanted to sing, but the thought of him chasing around the wilderness trying to catch a band of ruthless outlaws made her shudder. Did she really want a strong attachment to a lawman who was constantly in danger?

Jacob took Harry Clyde's little hat from the rack and settled it on his head. "Going to help Papa with the chores tonight?"

Harry Clyde nodded so hard his whole body jiggled.

Jacob laughed and said to Polly, "We'll be back." He carried his son out the back door.

Polly came to Ava's side and slipped an arm around her waist.

"Don't worry, dear."

"I try not to," Ava said, "but whenever I think about those bandits, it scares me."

"That's how I used to be. Now it seems you're worrying about Joe the same way I used to about Jacob whenever he was out of sight."

Ava gazed at Polly, who always seemed joyful, even when her husband was on the road driving a stagecoach.

"How do you do it, when Jacob's away?"

Polly gave her a little squeeze. "I've come to where I've stopped fretting. It's not as dangerous as it used to be for stage drivers, and if anything is going to happen to him, I certainly can't stop it. I have to trust God for his safety."

"That's true," Ava said, "and Jacob is a quick thinker. I'm sure if he has trouble, he finds a way out of it."

"Yes, like the time his stage was stranded in a blizzard and some of the passengers were injured."

"You wrote me about that."

"Your Joe is no slouch in that department, either."

Ava opened her mouth to protest at her designation of "your Joe," but she snapped her jaws shut. Maybe she was starting to think of him that way. Hard to believe she had met him less than a fortnight ago, and yet he meant so much to her.

Polly went to the cupboard for a stack of plates. "It's hard not to worry, but I can't think about it all the time. I don't know how to say this without sounding pious, but—"

"You, pious?" Ava chuckled. "A woman as jolly as you would never be thought pious."

"All right, then take this in the spirit it's meant: I give thanks for every day I've had Jacob, and I hope we get many more, but if not, we've had a wonderful time together. It's men like him and Joe who have made this country safe for families."

"I suppose you're right—men like your father, too, and all the railroad men and wagon masters before them, and lawmen and ranchers. . ."

"This territory is full of brave men." Polly began to set the table.

Ava couldn't help wondering if Joe was with the lawmen trying to catch the robbers. Rather than voice her thoughts, she decided to follow Polly's example. She sent up a prayer for Joe and the men he worked with and then tried to put it out of her mind.

A knock sent her to the front door. She opened it and stared in surprise at Joe.

"Come in," Ava cried. "I'm so glad to see you. We thought you might be off with the marshal, chasing robbers."

"Not me this time," Joe said. "I just came in on the train from Salt Lake City. I understand the outlaws have gotten away again though."

Polly stood in the kitchen doorway, wiping her hands on her apron. "That's a shame."

"Yes," Joe said. "Every time a posse trails them into the hills, they lose them. I'm afraid we've got to catch them red-handed."

Ava wasn't sure she liked the sound of that. The desperados would be more likely to shed blood if they were cornered.

"Well, come on in," Polly said cheerfully. "You're just in time for supper."

A week later, Joe set out on what might be his most dangerous assignment yet. The lawmen's earlier attempts to catch up with the band of robbers had come to nothing. He had managed two visits to Ava in between his stints for the railroad, but depending on how things went today, he might not see her for several days.

He mounted his horse and rode after Detective Simms. He was joining a posse of eight railroad policemen determined to catch the train robbers. Tonight's westbound train was carrying a load of silver to a bank in Salt Lake City. Concealing that knowledge had proved impossible, and any number of people seemed to have been on hand when the specie was loaded in St. Louis. Mr. Colson, Joe's boss in Cheyenne, had received a telegram asking for extra men to be on guard when the train came through.

The train itself carried a dozen officers, riding with the treasure all the way from St. Louis, and several men had switched out at stops in the larger towns along the way. But west of Cheyenne, the open plains offered many miles of track through unpopulated country, where a robbery could be pulled off with impunity—and thousands of square miles of wilderness into which a gang of outlaws could disappear and never be found.

Colson had sent out posses before, but they had not been successful so far. They'd had eight robberies in various places since the beginning of the year. The increased losses to the railroad as well as the passengers' fears spurred the railroad's management to get rid of the outlaw gangs.

Still anticipating his first month's pay, Joe was riding a borrowed horse and carrying weapons loaned to him by his boss and Simms. He patted the bay gelding's neck and urged him to keep pace with the others.

They rode westward from Cheyenne, leaving the station thirty minutes before the train was due there. Several officers would be on hand while the train was stopped at the Cheyenne depot. Joe and the others with him would be waiting in case the robbers tried to stop the locomotive west of town. He and his fellow policemen knew the robbers could have planted confederates on the train, but no matter where the robbery took place, they would have to have cohorts waiting with horses to make their escape. The mounted officers rode beside the tracks for ten miles, when Simms signaled for them all to stop.

"Rest your horses, men. That train should have left Cheyenne by now. It will catch up to us soon."

"I haven't seen any signs of the outlaws," one of the other men said.

Simms nodded. "I doubt that gang would hold up the train so close to Cheyenne, but you never know." He pulled out his watch and looked at it. "If it passes us on schedule, we'll follow along."

"Should we scout the tracks ahead?" the man named Farris asked, gazing down the tracks westward.

"Yes, you and Logan go," Simms said.

Joe was glad to keep moving, instead of doing nothing while they waited for the train. He and Farris loped their horses a half mile, gaining the top of a rise from which they could see down into a slight dip in the prairie.

"What's that?" Joe pointed ahead at a dark blur on the tracks.

Farris's jaw dropped. "They've blocked the tracks. Put some logs on them."

"Logs?" Joe looked around at the treeless grassland.

"They must have hauled them out here in a wagon. Come on, we've got to tell Simms!"

They raced back along their path and began waving their hats when the posse came into view. Simms and the others loped their horses toward Joe and Farris.

"Obstruction on the tracks," Farris yelled.

Simms hauled back on his reins and fumbled to take a red flag from the cantle of his saddle. He handed it to Farris just as they heard the eerie whistle of the locomotive in the distance.

"Flag the train," Simms told Farris. "We'll try to clear it."

Joe didn't wait but turned his horse and galloped back toward the knoll. As they began to ride down into the depression, Simms's horse pounded up beside him.

"Hold on, Logan! The robbers are probably waiting nearby. I don't want to get you killed."

Joe slowed his mount to a trot and watched the skyline. Any fold in the open land could hide a dozen horsemen.

One of the posse members yelled and pointed. Half a dozen riders appeared on the next hill, streaking away across the prairie.

"It's the gang," one of the detectives shouted.

"Go," Simms called to him, waving him and four other men on. "Logan, you're with me. Quick, now!"

Joe followed Simms, whose horse cannoned down the hill to where three sizable logs lay across the steel rails. Both jumped from the saddle and ran to the logs. The smallest was about eight feet long and six inches thick. Each seized one end and carried it off the tracks. The train's whistle blew, closer.

"Think they saw Farris in time?" Joe asked, panting, as they went back to try to move the next log. It was a couple of inches thicker.

"I don't know," Simms said. "Come on, put your back into it."

The squeal and screech of the train's brakes seemed almost on top of them as they rolled the second log off. Their horses snorted and galloped away from the tracks. Joe looked back the way they had come. The locomotive had crested the knoll and was rolling toward them amid a thunderous noise and the release of a big cloud of steam.

"We can do it," he yelled to Simms, and they both heaved the last log from the tracks as the engine reached them. It had slowed considerably but did not completely halt until the cowcatcher on the front was a hundred feet past them. Farris's horse galloped toward them, with Farris holding the red flag beneath one arm.

Joe and Simms stood panting beside the logs while two men climbed down from the second passenger car and walked toward them. Farris reined in his horse and waited with them.

"Detective Simms, is that you? What's going on?" one of the men called when they were close.

Simms waved. "Hello, Peters. The outlaws had blocked the tracks. We weren't sure we could clear it in time, so we had Farris flag you down. Good thing, too. If the engineer hadn't started to brake when he did, we wouldn't have made it, and you'd have derailed."

"Takes a long time to stop these things," Detective Peters agreed.

The train's conductor came toward them from the first passenger car. "Everything all right?"

Simms nodded. "Now it is. A posse's gone after the gang that was hiding out here waiting for you. Tell the engineer you can proceed. No one should bother you for the rest of this run. Sorry we had to stop you."

"It's better than the alternative," the conductor said. He waved and turned toward the locomotive.

"We'd better get back on board," Detective Peters said. "You'll wire on down the line and let us know if you catch them?"

"I expect Mr. Colson will spread the word, whatever happens," Simms said.

Peters and his companion climbed the steps to the passenger car's platform and waved. Joe, Farris, and Simms waited until the engineer got the train moving again.

"I'll go see if I can catch your horses now." Farris jogged his bay over the nearest rise.

"I hope we can catch up with the posse," Joe said. "I'd sure like to be there when they catch that bunch of robbers."

Chapter 7

Ava sat down to write to her parents. Her heart was in turmoil, in spite of her determination to remain calm like Polly. She mustn't let her agitation show through in her letter.

> Dear Pa and Mama,
>   I am having the most wonderful time with Polly and Jacob and the children. The Independence Day celebration was done up in grand style, and if not quite as elaborate as yours, I guarantee it was more enthusiastic. The horse races and shooting matches drew out the entire city, I'm sure.

She hesitated and dipped her pen in the ink again.

Do you remember the man I told you about from the train? Mr. Logan? Well, he has stopped here in Cheyenne. When outlaws stole the parcel he was to deliver, he had no need to go on, and he has taken a job with the railroad police. He drew sketches of two train robbers for them, and that was instrumental in the capture of one of the thieves. Apparently the railroad officials were impressed by Mr. Logan's observation skills, and he is training to be a detective. He went to Jacob's stagecoach depot one evening and came home with him for supper and has been to visit since. He is coming by again tomorrow.

Ava reread what she had written. Had she shown too much partiality for Mr. Logan—or Joe, as he had bid her call him? Her parents would surely read between the lines and see that she admired the man. She decided that was better than waiting to see if the acquaintance blossomed into more and then springing it on them. She let the paragraph stand but moved on to more mundane topics.

She had barely finished her letter when Harry Clyde entered the parlor, rubbing his eyes.

"Well, hello, young sir," Ava said, rising. "Did you have a good nap?"

Harry Clyde shook his head but came to her and allowed her to take him up into her arms.

"Shall we go find your mama?" Ava asked. "I think she's out back, hanging clothes."

The little boy nodded and buried his head in her shoulder.

In the backyard, Polly grinned as she pinned one of Amelia's diapers to the clothesline.

"Hello! Is Amelia up, too?"

"Still sleeping," Ava said. She walked over with Harry Clyde and looked in the clothes basket. Half a load of wet laundry still awaited attention. "Why don't you take Harry in for his snack, and I'll finish this."

"I can do it," Polly replied, reaching for another diaper.

"Of course you can, but I want to."

After a little more persuasion on Ava's part, Polly and her son headed inside. The sunshine felt good on Ava's shoulders as she hung up the rest of the wash. A soft wind blew from the west, and when her basket was empty, she walked along the line feeling the clean clothes. At the far end, she found quite a few items from an earlier washing that were dry, and she took them down and folded them into the basket.

When she stepped into the kitchen, Polly and Harry Clyde were sitting at the kitchen table with a plate of cookies between them. Harry's glass of milk was half empty, and Polly had a cup of hot tea at her place.

"My, you're industrious," Polly said when she saw the clean laundry. "I poured you some tea. Hope it's not too cool."

"That looks lovely." Ava set down the basket and took her place at the table. She reached for one of the cookies she and Polly had baked the day before.

"Those are so good," Polly said, taking another. "I'm glad you remembered your mother's recipe."

"She always made the best sugar cookies," Ava agreed.

"Well, I held some back for you and Joe to have when he calls tomorrow evening, and I expect there will be some pie left from dinner, too."

Ava smiled and took a sip of her tea. If only she could be as optimistic as Polly. Instead, she had mentally added, "*If* he calls tomorrow evening."

"What?" Polly asked.

"Nothing."

"Now, Ava, are you still fretting about Joe?"

"I can't forget what Jacob said about the trains."

"That last robbery wasn't anywhere near here."

"I know, but. . ." Ava shook her head.

Polly frowned. "If you're going to marry a policeman—"

"Whoa," Ava cried. "Who said anything about marrying him?"

Her friend laughed. "I've seen the way you look at each

other. Marriage is the logical conclusion."

"But. . .I'm only here for a month." Ava realized how quickly July was fleeing. "On August third, I'm to board the train back to Massachusetts."

"Are you?" Polly asked, as if it were the furthest thing from her mind.

"Yes, and it's coming right up."

Amelia's cry sounded from the bedroom. Polly took a quick sip of her tea and set the cup down. "I must get your sister now, Harry Clyde. You can entertain Aunt Ava for a few minutes."

Joe followed instructions when he reached the site of the standoff. Simms had picked up tips from a rancher and a freighter along the way as to where the outlaws had headed, with the posse in hot pursuit. When they found the other railroad police outside an old sod house, they dismounted and secured their horses with the rest. The men fanned out to surround the hideout and waited for a signal from their leader.

Joe's mouth went dry. He glanced to his left. He could see Farris crouched in the tall grass, and beyond him, Joe caught a glimpse of another railroad man's hat.

In the distance, Simms yelled, "You're surrounded by police. Come on out."

In answer, a volley of gunshots came from the soddy. A

rapid exchange of fire followed, after which smoke hung in the air and the prairie seemed oddly quiet.

"You listen to me now," Simms yelled. "We've got you surrounded, and we're not leaving. In fact, we've got more men on the way. If you want to sit it out, by nightfall we'll have a hundred men here. You're not getting away. Ever. So, you think about that. Any time you want to come out peacefully, you let us know, and we'll hold our fire."

Joe wasn't really sure how it happened, but thirty minutes later Simms convinced the men inside to throw down their guns and come out. While the others bound the prisoners and prepared to take them back to Cheyenne, Joe helped Simms search the soddy. Under a couple of the mattresses they found small pouches of money.

"Well, what do you know?" Simms was poking beneath one of the bunks, and he brought out a small cracker tin.

"Anything in it?" Joe asked.

"Let's see." Simms lifted the lid. "Ha. Jewelry. Must be stuff they haven't had a chance to sell yet." He carried the tin to the doorway so he could examine the contents in the sunlight.

"May I see?" Joe went to stand beside him. A jumble of rings, brooches, and pendants lay in the tin, along with two pocket watches and a military medal. Joe lifted one of the watches and opened it. "I think this is mine. They stole it off me the day I came to Cheyenne."

"Take it," Simms said.

"Don't I have to make a report or something?"

"Tell Colson when we get back to town, and he can mark it off his list."

"All right." Joe pocketed the watch and picked out a necklace. "Are these garnets?"

"I'd say so," Simms replied.

"Then this could be the necklace my employer wanted me to take to San Francisco. He said garnet and marcasite."

"Those things that look like tiny little diamonds are probably the marcasite," Simms said. "There's an earring like it." He pointed.

Joe plucked the earring from the trove. "Is there another one? He said there were earrings that matched the pendant."

"Here, you paw through it." Simms thrust the tin into his hands. "I'll make sure everyone's ready to head out."

Joe followed Simms slowly, poking through the glittering jewelry with one finger. He was rewarded by the sight of the second earring turning face upward to wink at him. With a sigh he took it out and wrapped it in his handkerchief with the necklace and second earring. A little more exploration revealed a diamond bracelet. He wasn't positive about this one, but it might be the other item with which Mr. Becker had entrusted him. He folded it up with the other items and slipped the handkerchief into the inner pocket of his jacket then closed the tin and hurried after Simms.

Two hours later, when the robbers were locked up and the men were writing their reports, he showed the items to Mr. Colson.

"So you think that's what was in the package they took from you last week?"

"I do, sir," Joe said. "I've checked it against the message the attorney, Mr. Becker, sent me, and they fit the description. With your permission, I could wire him and ask for a few more details."

"Go ahead, but if it's his we'll send him a bill for the telegrams."

Joe nodded. "If this is the right stuff, I don't think he'll mind. What will they do with all these other things if no one claims them?"

Colson shrugged. "We keep recovered loot for a year or so, and then, if we can't find the owners, we sell it. There's a bunch in the safe now that's due to be sold."

When Joe returned later with Becker's assurance that he had found the right jewelry, Mr. Colson opened the safe to get it out for Joe.

"He wondered if I could go on and deliver it for him," Joe told his boss. "I wasn't sure, since I just took this job. I'd come right back, though."

"San Francisco?" Mr. Colson said. "I guess so. You'd only be gone a few days, and you could work the trains going and coming."

Joe smiled. "That would be great."

Colson laughed. "Not every day you get paid by two employers at once, eh, Logan?"

He picked up another box that had been in the safe. "Here's the stuff we've collected that's never been claimed. Want to see it?"

"Sure."

When Colson opened the box, Joe caught his breath. One gem twinkled at him as though crying out for him to pick it up. Carefully, he took out the ring and gazed at the lovely blue stone. The round-cut sapphire was encircled by small diamond chips—or maybe more of the marcasite he'd seen on the garnet set, but these looked brighter.

"Pretty, isn't?" Colson said.

"It makes me think of the blue moon," Joe confessed. He hoped Colson wouldn't notice the flush heating his cheeks. "How much do you think it will sell for?"

"I don't know. I guess I can ask the jeweler down the street. You fancy it?"

"Well. . ." Joe chuckled. "There is someone I had in mind who might like it."

Ava opened the door at the Tierneys' house to find Joe on the doorstep. She didn't try to hide her relief or her pleasure at seeing him.

"You're back! I hope the other men are safe."

"Nobody was hurt, and we caught the robber gang."

"Wonderful!" She drew him inside and closed the door. "Won't you come into the kitchen and tell Polly and Jacob? I know they'll want to hear all about it."

"Certainly, but first, there's something I'd like to say to you, Ava."

"Oh?" She turned to face him. Joe was watching her intently, and she felt her cheeks warm under the scrutiny of his clear blue eyes. "What is it?"

"We found the things that were stolen from me on the trip out here."

Ava clutched his hand for a moment then drew back, embarrassed by her own enthusiasm. "I'm so glad."

"Me, too. I'll be making a quick trip to San Francisco, to deliver them for Mr. Becker, but I'll be back in just a few days. And before I go. . ." He hesitated and gazed into her eyes.

Ava felt her heart quicken.

"The moon is full tonight," Joe said. "It's the blue moon."

"So it is. I'd forgotten."

He drew in a deep breath. "Would you like to step outside and see it? It's rising over the prairie, and it's a fine sight."

"I. . .all right." Ava took Polly's blue knitted shawl from the back of a chair and slipped it around her shoulders. They walked out into the front yard, and Joe pointed. The moon, plump and full, was peeking from behind the edge of a fluffy cloud near the bell tower on the church down the street.

Ava gazed at it for a long moment and sighed. "You're right, it's beautiful."

"I suppose it would be prettier if we had a big old maple tree and we could stare at it through the branches."

"Do you think you'll miss the trees?" Ava asked. "That's what Polly said she missed most when she moved out here."

"I probably will. But I've been living in town the last few years, so it won't be as if I've come right from the middle of a forest." Joe chuckled. "It doesn't look particularly blue, does it?"

"Not especially."

"Ava, I—"

"Yes?" She turned to face him.

Joe reached into his pocket and took out something that gleamed in the moonlight. "I had an opportunity to buy this today, and I couldn't bear to think of it going to anyone but you."

He placed it in her hand, and she held it up. A ring. She caught her breath. What could he mean by it?

"If the light were better, you could see it's a sapphire. It made me think of the blue moon, which made me think of you. Ava, I know we haven't known each other long, and—and I'm not very good at this, but I love you, and well. . .out here it seems a little foolish to wait a long time, so I'm asking you now. Will you marry me?"

Ava realized she was staring at him and lowered her gaze to the ring again.

"If you'd like time to think about it," he began after a short pause.

"No, I don't need time. I think we shall get along splendidly."

"Really?"

"Yes." She looked up at him and smiled. "I wouldn't make you wait for another blue moon, Joe."

He leaned down and kissed her lightly then with more purpose.

Ava leaned against him for a moment. "Perhaps we should go inside and show Polly and Jacob," she whispered.

"I'm sure we should. Would you like to put it on first?"

"Yes." She let him slide the band over her finger and laughed. "I can't wait to see it in good light. Come on."

Later that evening, when Joe had gone, Ava was too wound up to sleep. She sat down to write a letter to her parents. The moonlight shone through the window, so bright she didn't even need to light the lamp.

> *Dear Pa and Mama,*
>
> *I have some news for you, and I hope it makes you happy. On this rare blue moon, an even rarer thing happened to me. You remember Mr. Logan, the man from the train? Well, he*

wishes to become your son-in-law.

Ava reread the paragraph and smiled. She spread her hand and gazed at the sapphire ring and then dipped her pen in the inkwell.

> *We wondered if you would like to come out here for the wedding. If not, Joe and I will save until we have enough to travel back there. He said the railroad will discount our tickets. I shall write more soon, but I couldn't wait for you to hear. Your loving daughter,*
> *Ava*

Susan Page Davis is the author of more than fifty novels in the romance, mystery, suspense, and historical romance genres. A Maine native, she now lives in western Kentucky with her husband, Jim, a retired news editor. They are the parents of six, and the grandparents of nine fantastic kids. She is a past winner of the Carol Award, the Will Rogers Medallion for Western Fiction, and the Inspirational Reader's Choice Award. Susan was named Favorite Author of the Year in the 18th Annual Heartsong Awards. Visit her website at: www.susanpagedavis.com.

THE DOGWOOD BLOSSOM BRIDE

Miralee Ferrell

Chapter 1

Gracie Addison bit her lip to keep it from trembling— from anger rather than a desire to cry. Of all the tomfool things she'd ever heard of, this had to be the worst. She gave a light stamp of her foot, hoping her father would take her seriously for a change. "I have no interest whatsoever in Jerold Carnegie. I'm not cut out to be a high-and-mighty society lady, married to a politician." She flicked a finger at her trousers and dusty boots, peeking out from under the rolled cuffs.

Her father snorted his disapproval and leaned his arm against the mantel in the drawing room of their spacious home. "Exactly my point. You need to cease wearing those ridiculous costumes and utilize the manners your mother taught you before her death. If she had lived past your ninth birthday, she would be horrified at some of the choices you've made."

"Oh, posh, Father. Of all the people in my life, she understood my tomboy tendencies better than anyone. I'd think by now you'd be used to how I dress and the things I do."

He straightened, and a frown pulled at the corners of his normally cheerful mouth. "She understood when you were nine, but she would not have approved at nineteen. It is high time you act like a lady. Climbing trees and riding astride, not to mention wading into the creek to set traps for fish and any of the other numerous things you do, aren't becoming. I want you to marry well, and Jerold Carnegie will succeed in this world. He's a good man with an excellent reputation. What could you possibly have against him?"

Gracie rolled her eyes. "He's boring. B-O-R-I-N-G. He doesn't have a particle of humor in his dry bones, and his mustache twitches at the slightest provocation. Besides, you're doing a fine job caring for me. So whatever do I need with Mr. Carnegie?"

His shoulders slumped. "Has it ever occurred to you that you are my only child, and as such, I would appreciate you carrying on our family line?"

Gracie forced herself to relax her tense posture and stepped forward to give her father a hug. "I'm sorry for arguing. But I truly have no interest in Mr. Carnegie, and I see no need to rush into marriage."

His eyes closed for a brief moment then opened, and the corner of his lips tipped up. "All I ask is that you try, Gracie. To please me, if for no other reason. I have invited Mr. Carnegie to supper tonight, and I will expect you to dress and act the lady I know you can be. He is new enough in town not to have gotten wind of your antics yet—please, give yourself a chance to get acquainted."

She pressed her lips together and tried not to smile. Only last week the man in question had come upon her on the outskirts of town while she was riding her horse astride and wearing trousers. In spite of that start, she'd still glimpsed a flicker of interest in the man's eyes. Somehow she'd have to find a way to quell that.

Mr. Carnegie wasn't altogether horrid. He was simply unappetizing—like a bowl of day-old bread soaked in milk when she hungered for steak. But she did hate to disappoint her father. "All right. I'll be here for supper, but don't expect anything more."

He grinned and started to reply, but she shook her head. "I mean it. I'll be polite, but that's all. And now I'm going to go for a walk." Gracie pivoted and waltzed out of the room, humming a tune. Maybe she could position herself in a tree that Mr. Carnegie would ride beneath on his way to their home and discourage his attentions.

She hid a smirk. The sight would shock him so much he wouldn't return.

Will Montgomery slumped in the saddle, weary and glad to have finally reached the outskirts of Goldendale. He glanced behind him to check on his eight-year-old niece, Laura. She had withstood the journey better than he had. The three-day-long winding climb up the Columbia Hills from The Dalles was enough to tire man and horse alike, but it wouldn't have been so bad if he'd slept last night. A cougar screaming in the distance had kept him patrolling the area in front of the fire.

It hadn't awakened Laura, but he couldn't take a chance the big cat would spot the little girl and decide she was an easy meal. The only things he wanted now were to get to Curt Warren's home, see the child settled, and roll into bed. He twisted in his saddle and watched the bright-eyed girl riding her horse like she'd stepped into the saddle only an hour before. "Are you all right, Laura?"

She nodded and grinned. "I'm getting kind of sore, but I don't mind. I just wish I could wear trousers like you."

"We'll be there soon, and you can rest." He smiled to himself. Laura was so like her mother, Karen. Pain shot through his chest at the memory of his sister who had died an unnecessary death.

He pushed the thought away. His new boss didn't expect him to start work right away, so he'd have a few days to settle in before tackling his new profession. He was thankful for the job, but it was a far cry from the life of a cowboy he'd lived for the better part of his adult years. He hated giving up his life on the range, but it was time to find something that would provide a decent living—especially if he ever hoped to find a wife and settle down.

He scowled. Not that he'd had much luck in that direction. Lucinda, the last girl he'd thought he cared for enough to marry had been nothing but a flirt. Something he hadn't discovered until she'd dropped him for a newspaperman with aspirations of bigger and better things than a cowboy could ever attain.

He wanted a woman like his mother had been—feminine and faithful to her man and her home. Looking back, Will felt as though he'd been saved from a bad marriage. Lucinda had sworn she'd never look at another man when they'd met, and he'd believed her.

Until Reed Jenkins waltzed into town. No, a solid girl with her head on her shoulders was what he needed, and he wouldn't settle for anything less.

Will came to a fork in the road and reined his horse to a stop under a flowering dogwood. If he remembered correctly, the Warren home and woodworking shop were to the right, but he'd better reread the directions in Curt's letter.

Will kept one hand on the reins and reached around with the other to his saddlebag. He fumbled with the buckle but finally got it open. As he searched inside, something overhead in the widespread branches of the dogwood tree rustled the leaves, and a shower of pink blossoms cascaded onto his shoulders. Dusty, his dapple-gray gelding, snorted but didn't move.

The branches close above his head shifted and swayed, and two trouser-clad legs with boots beneath dangled above Dusty's nose. The horse bolted forward, making Laura's horse snort and shy.

Will tightened the reins and brought the startled horse to a stop. "Laura. Calm your horse, then get off."

He waited until the girl obeyed; then he swung Dusty around and heeled him forward, halting him directly under the small boots. Definitely a youngster, but one who needed to be more careful. "Hey you. Boy. Come down here."

A gasp and then a titter sounded above him, but no one answered.

"This isn't funny. You can't go around swinging from trees and spooking horses. My niece nearly got hurt."

Even the birds that had been scolding from branches high up in the neighboring tree had stilled their chatter, but the boy didn't respond. In fact, one leg slowly withdrew until the top of the boot began to disappear into the foliage.

"Oh no you don't." Will stood in his stirrups and grasped the other dangling leg just above the boot. "You aren't going to get off that easy." He kept a tight grip on the boy and released his reins. He grabbed the other leg at the knee and yanked.

Gracie felt the strong grip on her leg and gasped once again as she almost lost her grip on the tree. This was most definitely not Jerold Carnegie. She had no idea who it might be, as she'd never heard his voice before, but the man seemed determined to dislodge her from her perch. She held on to the branch above her with all her might.

How humiliating—and a bit frightening—to be yanked from a tree by a stranger—or by anyone, for that matter. Gracie's cheeks burned. And he thought her a boy who'd purposely spooked his horse. She'd been daydreaming and hadn't even realized the man had stopped under her tree, or she'd not have allowed her feet to dangle.

It had been a foolish whim to try to shock Mr. Carnegie and scare him off from wanting to court her, and she'd changed her mind minutes ago. She'd climbed to the lowest branch possible with the intention of jumping down and heading home. Maybe her father was right, and it was time she gave up such foolishness.

If only she could get a better grip and climb high enough in the dogwood to keep from being found out by this stranger. Her heart thumped hard in her chest. What would he do to her if he caught her?

He yanked on her legs again, and her grasp on the limb

loosened. Perspiration slicked her palms. She wanted to demand the man release her, but speaking would give her away. She kicked one boot, trying to loosen his grasp and instead connected with a solid object.

He groaned.

Oh dear. Had she kicked the man's head? Well, it served him right for being rough. "Let go of me, you lout!"

His hold relaxed for a second, and Gracie made one last effort to heave herself higher into the branches. Pink dogwood blossoms drifting from the shivering tree clouded her vision.

"No you don't, you young scamp. First you spook our horses, then you boot me in the noggin. I ought to whip you when I get you down, but I'll satisfy myself with presenting you to your pa and letting him do the honors."

The hands gripping her legs tightened like steel bands. Gracie hadn't known a man could contain such strength. As the horse danced around beneath the tree, a mighty heave from below tore Gracie's fingers from her hold. She plummeted down—right into the arms of the most handsome man she'd ever hoped to see.

Chapter 2

Will tightened his grip to keep from dropping the young woman he'd been certain was a boy, although she didn't weigh as much as a bag of feathers. He gazed into the wide green eyes staring up into his, and took in the passel of red-gold hair that had come out of its binding. One wayward lock blew across his lips, causing a shiver to run down his spine. He reached for the tendril, not sure what he'd do with it when captured but completely enthralled at the touch.

"Uncle Will, who is that?" Laura's high-pitched voice behind him almost made him lose his hold and drop the young woman.

The redhead clutched at his shirt collar, and dark color flooded her face. "Put me down this instant." She swiveled her head, trying to see over his shoulder. "I don't care to be embarrassed in front of your wife and child."

"Wife and child?" Will shifted the woman's weight a bit, and his lips quirked. "My niece, Laura, is the only one with me, and I doubt she cares one way or the other about what happened."

Laura tugged her horse forward and turned her round eyes on the woman. "Why were you in that tree?"

Some of the stiffness went out of the woman, but she glared at him rather than answer Laura's question. "I will not talk to anyone while in this position—not even a child. Let go of me, or I shall make things quite unpleasant for you."

Will chuckled and shook his head. "I doubt a little mite like you could do much harm, but I'll put you down. Swing your feet over to one side, and I'll let you slip to the ground. Don't want you to fall and hurt yourself."

She did as he said, her boots hitting the ground with barely a whisper. She crossed her arms and took a step back. "I do not appreciate being laughed at or manhandled—or taken for a boy. Whatever did you pull me out of that tree for, anyway?"

Laura tugged on her horse's reins and walked closer to the woman. "What's your name?"

"Gracie Addison."

All the stuffing seemed to go out of the woman when she spoke to Laura, leaving her looking more like a vulnerable child than an adult. But that didn't last long. She swung toward him, her fists planted on her hips and eyes narrowed. "I want an answer to my questions, along with your name, mister."

Will grinned, which seemed to make her madder. "Will Montgomery, ma'am, at your service." He swept off his hat and gave a short bow. He probably should climb off his horse and introduce himself proper-like, but from the looks of the little dynamo on the ground, she'd light into him like a wild bull at branding time. No, sir, he was safer staying on his horse.

"And like I said, this is my niece, Laura, who is in my care. As to why I pulled you out of that tree, I told you. You spooked my horse then kicked me in the noggin. I thought you were a boy out to pull a prank." He raised his brows and chuckled. "You can't blame a man for making a mistake when you dress like that and climb trees. What are you, all of fifteen or sixteen?"

Gracie clamped her teeth on a cry of frustration. She'd shout at the insufferable man if it wasn't for the wide-eyed child taking in every word that passed between them. Fifteen or sixteen, was she? "I'll have you know, Mr. Montgomery, that I am nineteen, and what I wear or choose to do is no concern of yours. Why should I quit doing something I love?" She crossed her arms and tilted her chin.

He shook his head, but the smile that both irritated and drew her lingered on those finely carved lips. In fact, his entire face was bathed in laugh lines as though he could barely contain himself. He swept off his hat, revealing brown curls that reflected a hint of gold in the sunlight, and the movement caused his shirt to tighten over the broad, well-built shoulders she'd gripped only moments before. "Why, I reckon most women your age are too busy trying to entice a man to marry them to care for such childish things as climbing trees."

Gracie glowered at him—a cowboy if ever she'd seen one—but there were no big cattle ranches in their area, so what was he doing here? She narrowed her eyes. "Climbing trees is far from childish." She directed her attention to the little girl with the long blond braid and dimpled cheeks. "Do you like trees, Miss Laura?"

The girl giggled. "I'm not a miss. My name is just Laura. I've never climbed a tree. Uncle Will won't let me. Maybe you can teach me."

Gracie stifled a gasp so as not to startle the child. "Why-ever not?" She stared at the offending uncle. Why would anyone deny a child such a wholesome pastime?

He stiffened, and his face lost the happy light as quickly as if water had been thrown on a candlewick. "Come, Laura. Mr. and Mrs. Warren are probably wondering why we haven't arrived yet. And we certainly don't want to keep Miss Addison from her—activities."

He arched a brow and waited until Laura mounted. "Nice to meet you, ma'am"—he reached out and snagged the reins of her horse—"and I certainly hope you don't kick the wrong man in the head while swinging from your next tree."

The horses trotted down the path at the fork, their riders' backs to Gracie and the man's gruff response still ringing in her ears. The nerve, talking to her like a silly child. She shivered as she rubbed the spot where his hand had clamped on her arm to keep her from falling after she'd landed in his lap, conflicted by the strange emotions that battled for dominance.

Then she remembered Laura's words—her uncle wouldn't let her climb a tree—and irritation won out over the surprising melting sensation she'd experienced while held in his arms. He'd said they were headed to the Warren home. Word was out that Curt Warren had hired a new woodworking apprentice since his business had grown and his wife had given birth to twins. It appeared Will Montgomery might not be a cowpoke after all, although he didn't look or act like any carpenter she'd ever met.

All children needed to experience a full life outdoors, whether it be wading in a creek, riding a horse, catching a fish just for the joy of the battle, or climbing a tree. She'd have to find a way that Laura Montgomery wouldn't miss out on her childhood, and hoped she didn't irritate the child's cranky uncle in the meantime.

Will had done all he could do to quiet Laura's protests as they rode away from the intriguing young woman he'd left standing under the dogwood tree a hundred yards back. He needed to think about what happened—or better yet, to shut out the vision of her tumbled red curls and green eyes so deep and vivid that a man could sink into their depths and never find his way back.

Once, he'd felt the same way with Lucinda. Her charm and beauty had swept him off his feet at first sight, but her beauty didn't penetrate to her core. Still he'd pursued her, ignoring the gentle warning that must have been sent from God, only to have his heart broken a few weeks later as he was fixing to propose. A pretty face didn't mean a thing, and Gracie Addison was more than pretty; she had a sharp tongue, to boot.

A pang of guilt smote him. In all fairness, he *had* yanked her from a tree and laughed at her when he'd thought her a silly girl. He guessed she'd had the right to set him straight. But it didn't mean he would be taken in by another attractive woman—and certainly not one so reckless as to put herself in danger.

An image of his sister's tragic death arose from long ago, and he shuddered, pushing it back into the dark cave of grief where it belonged. He'd meant it when he'd told Laura to stay out of trees, and Miss Daredevil had better not try to influence the girl.

"Laura, do you feel comfortable trotting for a bit? We're later than I expected after running into Miss Addison, and I'm afraid the Warrens will have supper ready."

She rolled her eyes and booted her horse into a slow trot—about the only speed the horse knew, and the reason he'd been purchased. "I'm not a baby, Uncle Will. You don't let me do anything fun. Why can't I wear trousers and have adventures like Miss Addison?"

"Because I said so, that's why." He snapped his lips shut and pressed them together. Laura would be safe and grow up to be a lady, if he had anything to say about it.

Chapter 3

Gracie stepped into the kitchen and eyed the huckleberry cobbler she'd baked yesterday. It was a little lopsided, but her father never seemed to mind. At least Jerold Carnegie had come down with a cold and had sent his regrets last night. It was enough that she'd had to put up with one insufferable man without coming home and being bored senseless by another.

Color rose to her cheeks as she suddenly realized how silly she must have looked to that handsome cowboy. A giggle started deep inside and forced its way out, and she pressed her fingers over her lips. Climbing trees was unusual for a young woman of her age, but she didn't normally care. It relaxed her when life got difficult, as it had of late with Father pressing her to consider marriage—and to Jerold Carnegie, of all people.

She'd been thinking of driving over to see Deborah Warren to help ease her burden—especially since her life had been exceedingly busy after giving birth to twins a little over a year and a half ago. Maybe they would enjoy the cobbler.

Gracie tried to convince herself she didn't care to bump into that bossy man again, but something inside was unsettled at the memory of his saucy grin and his arms around her. She sobered as she reconsidered the wisdom of seeing him again. But surely he'd be in Curt Warren's workshop, so she needn't talk to him. Besides, wasn't it more important to help Deborah if she needed it?

A few minutes later she reined her horse and buggy to a halt in front of the cozy cottage on the outskirts of town. The front door opened and Curt stepped onto the porch, wiping his hands on a dish towel, his brows almost meeting in the middle of his forehead. His face relaxed at the sight of her, and he hurried forward. "Gracie, how good to see you. Was Deborah expecting you?"

She shook her head and plucked the pan of cobbler off the seat beside her. "I thought I'd surprise her. With all the extra work she has since the twins arrived, I hoped she might enjoy a treat, so I baked a berry cobbler and brought it with me." She handed it to Curt then clambered down the one step and onto the ground beside him. "Maybe I can take over a few chores while I'm here if you need to return to your workshop."

Curt gave a short nod. "Thank you, but you might not want to stay once you're inside. I'm afraid things are a bit turbulent at the moment."

He escorted her onto the porch and through the front door, balancing the covered pan on one hand.

Gracie followed him across the tiny entry and halted in the doorway to the kitchen, gazing at the unexpected mess that had descended on what was normally a well-ordered room. Dishes littered the cupboard beside the washbasin, and a pot of hot water bubbled on the woodstove, putting steam into the already warm air. Deborah leaned over a chair trying to spoon food into a wailing girl's mouth while her towheaded brother banged his spoon on the floor where he sat sprawled in a puddle of spilled oatmeal.

Deborah looked up as a tear trickled down her flushed cheek. "Hello, Gracie. Please forgive the mess."

Curt rushed forward to set the cobbler on the table. He scooped the little boy off the floor. "Deb, you should be in bed. I told you I'd care for the children."

"They were crying, and you weren't in the house, so I decided to feed them. I feel a bit shaky, but I'm stronger than I was yesterday. I can help." She plucked a damp rag from the table and wiped the little girl's face.

Gracie held out her arms toward the toddler. "I can take

care of Samuel if you want to take Sarah and clean her up. It appears Deborah needs to go back to bed. I'm happy to stay and help." She bounced the boy on her hip. "I can put this room back to rights in no time." The child squealed in delight and reached a sticky hand up to pat Gracie's cheek, depositing a fair amount of the oatmeal.

The thud of boots on the back porch and the squeak of a door hinge swung Gracie around. Laura, the child she'd seen riding with her uncle, stepped into the room, followed by Will Montgomery. Gracie's heart gave a quick lurch. She met his eyes, and her heart rate settled into a rapid beat. He smiled as his gaze rested on her stained cheek, and warmth flooded her face. This man had already seen her in a poor light when they'd met—what must he think of her now?

She dipped her head. "Mr. Montgomery. I hope you've settled in all right?"

Deborah's lips parted as she looked from one to the other. "You've met Will?"

Gracie nodded. She didn't know whether to be pleased that he'd kept their meeting to himself, or disappointed that he hadn't thought enough of her to share with his hosts. "I. . .bumped into him on the road."

His brow raised, and the corner of his mouth quirked. "Yes, I'd say that was accurate."

Laura snickered and tugged at her uncle's sleeve. "You was holding her in your arms, Uncle Will."

His face sobered, and he leaned over to whisper something into her ear. Her grin faded, and she nodded. "I'm sorry, Miss Addison."

Gracie's mortification faded at the sight of the little girl's distress. "Please, don't worry about it, Laura. I think I'll clean Samuel up then help Deborah with the dishes. In fact, would you care to dry them for me?" She gave Laura a bright smile and was rewarded to see her expression clear.

Deborah swayed on her feet, and Curt caught her by the shoulders. He swung her into his arms. "That settles it. I'm putting you to bed this instant. You won't mind watching the children until I return, Gracie?"

"Not at all. I'm happy to help."

A knock sounded at the front door as Curt headed for the bedroom with Deborah. Gracie shifted Samuel to her other hip. "I'll get that."

Will stepped forward. "Allow me. You have your hands full." He swung around and strode down the short hall to the entry.

As his footsteps faded, Gracie tuned her hearing toward the front door. Whoever had arrived hadn't come in, but she could hear soft murmurs that sounded decidedly feminine. And where had Laura gotten to?

The little girl appeared in the doorway from the hall, her eyes wide. "My new teacher is talking to Uncle Will, and I think she likes him. She's smiling real big, and she's awful pretty with her cheeks all pink."

Gracie wanted to sink through the floor. Carissa Sanderson was her best friend, as well as being one of the prettiest and sweetest women she knew. She wouldn't blame Will Montgomery a bit if he was already smitten with Laura's new teacher. Then why did her heart hurt thinking about it? She tried to shake off the sensation and forced herself to smile at Laura. "Miss Sanderson is a wonderful teacher, and I'm certain you'll love her."

Laura nodded and took a step closer to Gracie. She hesitated, peeked over her shoulder toward the front room, then lowered her voice: "Would you teach me to climb trees and fish in the stream? That's the kind of teacher I want." She wrinkled her nose. "I don't care for school, not even if Uncle Will does like that teacher."

Gracie didn't know whether to gasp or laugh, but she settled for a smile. "I'll have to see what your uncle thinks. I can't imagine he'd mind you learning to fish, but I do remember him saying something about not wanting you to climb trees. Did you fall out of one and hurt yourself?"

Laura's expectant look faded, and she dropped her gaze to the floor. "No. I think Uncle Will's being mean. He doesn't want me to have any fun at all."

Compassion swept over Gracie, and she reached for the girl and pulled her close. "I'm sure that's not the case, sweetie. Tell you what—I'll do my best to teach you to fish and climb a tree—"

"Don't make promises you can't keep, Miss Addison."

Will stood in the doorway to the kitchen, his expression cool. "Laura, why don't you go play outside while I have a word with Miss Addison?"

Will worked to soften his tone and leaned his shoulder against the door frame. He wanted to stride forward and make sure this stubborn woman listened this time, but he wasn't an ogre and refused to act like one. "You were saying?"

She tilted her chin to the side and narrowed her eyes. "You are certainly quick to jump to conclusions, Mr. Montgomery. If you'd listened another few seconds you might have discovered what I planned to say to your niece, instead of assuming and scolding us both. I'm not a child. I'm as old as Carissa Sanderson and quite able to make my own decisions."

He straightened, all pretense of ease gone. "Not where my niece is concerned. And I'm not sure what Miss Sanderson has to do with anything. She seemed like she had a sensible head on her shoulders and acted every bit the lady. I expect she'll make a fine teacher for Laura."

Will wanted to bite his tongue after the words left his mouth. Why had the teacher been brought into the conversation? Of course, she was a nice enough young woman, and she certainly seemed capable. Gracie Addison, on the other hand—he couldn't even begin to say what he thought of her—a spitfire who appeared to take foolish chances with her life, but who cared enough to offer to help Deborah Warren and the children. Not to mention her fresh beauty, sparkling eyes, and the determined spirit she'd shown from the moment she dropped into his arms under that tree.

Gracie's face paled, and she took a step back. "Miss Sanderson is an excellent teacher, and yes, she's also a fine lady—unlike me. So don't worry, Mr. Montgomery, I won't taint your niece or lead her down a dangerous path. I'd already told her, before you interrupted, that she must have your permission for me to help her. Not that I understand your hesitation, but be that as it may, I'll not interfere."

If Will could kick himself across the kitchen and back, he'd do so. What an idiot he'd been—and now he'd hurt Miss Addison and implied he didn't believe her to be a lady. "I apologize, miss. It appears we've gotten off on the wrong foot. Again. And it's my fault." He extended his hand. "Friends?"

Gracie hesitated. Then she stepped toward him and smiled. "Friends." She placed her hand in his.

A shock of awareness jolted him so hard he almost dropped her hand. "Thank you." He gently squeezed the soft fingers before he released her. "I don't have to start work in the shop for a few days. How about I help you out here? It looks like you've taken on a big job, what with Deborah ill and the babies so fussy. I hope they aren't coming down sick, as well."

Gracie's eyes widened. "Aren't you worried about Laura? I think Deborah is mostly worn out and has a cold, but maybe you and Laura should stay somewhere else to be safe."

Will shook his head. "I promised Curt I'd start work sometime late next week. We were going to start sooner, but he wants to stay close to the house. Laura has always been incredibly healthy, and I'm not worried about myself." He grinned. "I meant what I said about helping. In fact, I'm not a bad cook. How about we get these dishes done and whip up some supper so Deborah can rest?"

Surprise registered on Gracie's face before she swiveled toward the sink. "All right, if you insist." She tossed a saucy grin over her shoulder. "I happen to be a terrible cook, so you'd better be able to stand behind your boast. What's your specialty?"

He chuckled and moved up beside her, snagging a dish towel from a hook nearby. "You wash and I'll dry?"

She giggled. "No specialty, huh? Just as I thought."

"Not what I said. I happen to prefer surprises, that's all. You'll have to stick around long enough to find out."

Her brows arched, and her lips opened when a shout from outside sounded through the open kitchen window.

"Uncle Will! Come see! I'm way up in the tree like Miss Gracie, and I can go even higher."

Will froze, his heart in his throat and fear gripping his

insides so hard he thought he'd double over and retch. He bolted from the room, his thoughts flashing to his dead, daredevil sister. "*Like Miss Gracie,*" Laura had said. He shouldn't have gotten friendly with Gracie Addison. He should have known better than to let Laura be influenced by her behavior, and now it could be too late.

Chapter 4

Gracie stood rooted to the floor, not comprehending what could possibly be the problem. Laura was climbing a tree, but Will had raced from the room as though some tragedy were about to occur. She knew he didn't want his niece climbing, but children had done so and taken tumbles, but rarely come to harm, for centuries. She wiped her damp hands on a towel and headed for the door. What could make a grown man anxious about something as innocent as climbing a tree?

She stepped outside and looked into the branches of the nearby maple. Will stood at the base looking up through the leaves, and Gracie could barely see Laura about fifteen feet from the ground.

Will gestured toward his niece. "Laura, I said come

down this minute. It's not safe to be that high, and you're going to tear your dress."

"No fair, Uncle Will! I'm not near as high as Miss Gracie was, and she didn't get hurt." Her high-pitched voice drifted through the leaves. "Please let me stay. I want to do fun things like she does. Please?"

"Come down this minute, Laura." His voice shook with intensity.

The leaves trembled as the little girl made her way down a few more feet until she was hardly out of his reach. Gracie moved closer, wondering at the tension stiffening Will's body. "Laura, honey, I know you're having fun, and you were very brave going so high, but it's time to come down." She raised her brows and smiled at Will but only got a glower in return.

"Don't encourage her." He hissed the words, and his eyes shot sparks. "Laura, come down to the next branch where I can lift you down the rest of the way."

"Nuh-uh." Laura's face peeked through the branches, and she scowled. "Gonna do it myself." She shimmied over to the trunk then wrapped her arms around it and stepped to the branch below. As her foot touched the branch, she released her hold with one hand and reached down to grasp the one below.

Will growled deep in his throat and walked toward a spot beneath her at the exact moment her foot slid off the branch and she pitched headlong toward the ground.

Will darted the last stride, his arms extended and his heart pounding in his chest like a blacksmith swinging a hammer against an anvil. He couldn't let anything happen to Laura. He clenched his jaw and snatched the girl out of the air before she hit the ground. He set her down gently and knelt in front of her. "Are you all right?"

She pulled back, her earlier scowl reappearing and deepening. "Why didn't you let me climb higher? You aren't fair to make me come down when I was having fun. Miss Gracie likes to climb trees, and she understands, don't you?" She swung her gaze to the silent young woman standing nearby.

Gracie stared at Laura then turned her attention on Will, her eyes soft and inquisitive.

A lump formed in Will's throat, but he pushed it down. He would not be influenced by a warm gaze, no matter how beautiful the woman. "I'm sure Miss Addison does understand, as she takes foolish chances herself, but that does not mean you are allowed to do so. You go straight to your room now and stay there until supper. You disobeyed me by climbing that tree, and you need to think about your actions."

"But Uncle Will—"

He placed his hands on her shoulders and gave a gentle shove. "Now, Laura." Hardening his heart against the sniffles coming from his niece as she tromped away, he turned toward Gracie. "This wouldn't have happened if she hadn't seen you in that tree."

She crossed her arms over her chest. "You're blaming me for your niece's misbehavior?" She shook her head. "You don't make a lick of sense, and as far as I can see, you're taking this too far. Laura was doing a very competent job until you demanded she come down and she scrambled to obey. If she'd taken her time, I'm certain she would have been fine."

Will closed his eyes as memories again flooded his mind. When he opened them, Gracie was staring at him with something like compassion shining on her captivating face. "Would you please come back inside so I can explain?"

She hesitated a moment then nodded. "A cup of coffee or tea sounds good. I saw Deborah had a pot on the stove."

He inclined his head but didn't reply. Why had he offered to explain? If only Gracie didn't turn out to be a flirt or untrustworthy like Lucinda—but what was he thinking? It wasn't as if he were planning on marrying Gracie. For some reason he couldn't explain, he wanted to tell her why he wouldn't allow Laura to attempt anything that smacked of danger. He didn't really know her, but something about Gracie Addison drew him at a deeper level than he'd ever felt before.

Gracie settled into a kitchen chair across the beautiful hand-crafted table Curt had built for Deborah and watched Will as he poured two mugs of coffee. The man still mystified her. Laughing and teasing one minute then scolding her for being a bad influence on his niece the next. She'd like to spurn whatever explanation he gave as irrational, after the way he'd acted outside. But being charitable and listening was the godly thing to do, even if it went against her natural inclination.

Will dropped into the chair across from her and took a drink of his coffee. He set the mug on the table. "I don't know what I was thinking to burden you with my problems."

Gracie blinked. This was not at all what she'd expected. Defiance, chastisement, even a bit of condescension, but certainly not humility or sorrow. She sat up straighter and laced her fingers on top of the table. "Please, Will. I'd like to hear whatever you have to say."

His brows arched. "You called me Will."

Warmth blossomed in her cheeks. "I'm sorry. I didn't mean to be forward."

"Not at all." He reached toward her but stopped a few inches short of her hand. "I can't deny I've been thinking of you as Gracie since you arrived today, in spite of my behavior to the contrary." He leaned back and let his hands fall into his lap. "Am I being too presumptuous?"

She waited half-a-dozen heartbeats, willing herself to breathe slowly. "I think I'd like that. Now please, go ahead. I promise I'll be respectful and listen."

"Thank you." He closed his eyes for a moment, and a flicker of what appeared to be pain contorted his brow. Finally, he opened his eyes and sucked in a long breath. "Laura's mother was my sister. She died a year ago, and it was all my fault. I killed my sister."

Chapter 5

Gracie bit her lip to keep from gasping. He'd killed his sister? Surely she'd heard wrong. "I don't understand...."

"No, I'm sure you don't. Let me back up to our childhood. Karen and I were always close as she was my only sibling. I was a year older and charged with watching out for her as we grew. The problem was, we were both daredevils, and Karen was quite the tomboy. She loved all the same things you do—riding astride, fishing, climbing trees, swimming in water too deep to be safe. She did it all. And I urged her on to take more risks with every new adventure we conquered. My pa would have skinned me alive if he'd known some of the things we attempted." A smile flickered across his lips, softening his strong jawline.

She leaned forward. "So you loved her? You have good memories."

"Yes. She was a wonderful sister, and I was the big brother who could do no wrong in her eyes. Then when she was only fifteen, she met Vernon, a man I didn't care for or trust. He stayed long enough to marry her, but when Laura was born, he disappeared and never returned. Karen was heartbroken, and I didn't think she'd ever come out of her despair. Then one day she was herself again, and more reckless than ever. I think she would have pushed herself too far, but for baby Laura. As the girl grew, Karen began to see she needed to slow down—to be careful and not foolhardy, even if her heart was broken."

The room quieted, and Gracie waited—she wanted to press him, wanted to understand, but she knew he'd continue when he was ready.

He shook himself like a bear coming out of hibernation, needing to shake off the effects of the long sleep. "Laura was at a neighbor's. I'd ridden with Karen to town—a wire had come in and she was fearful. Turns out a sheriff from another town sent word that her no-good husband got shot cheating at cards. She was numb—she went from defiant to despondent in a matter of seconds. All the way home, she could barely move her horse out of a walk. It was coming onto dark, and I urged her to hurry. 'Let's race,' I said, just to shake her out of her doldrums. Like when we were youngsters—I told her I'd beat her home—that she was too slow to beat me—but I planned to let her win.

"All of a sudden, she dug her spurs into her gelding's side and took off across the flat, running like demons were pursuing her—and I suppose in a way, they were." Will sucked in a harsh breath before he continued. "I stayed behind her, whooping and hollering like an idiot, thinking it would give her a chuckle. When all of a sudden—" He shuddered and put his face in his hands.

Gracie reached across the table and touched his fingers, not caring whether it was appropriate or if Curt might come into the room. Will gripped her hand as though it were a lifeline, but kept his eyes cast down at the table.

"All of a sudden, her horse stepped in a hole. Broke his leg and sent her flying. Her head hit a rock." He gave a harsh laugh. "Must have been the only big rock in a hundred yards, and she hit it. She was dead before I could get to her side. My fault. I killed her. If I hadn't pushed. . ."

Gracie could stand it no longer. She shoved her chair back and stood. "Shh. . . It wasn't your fault." She walked around the table and laid her hand on his shoulder. "You were trying to encourage her, but you didn't know what would happen. You were trying to help, to cheer her up. You can't blame yourself."

He raised red-rimmed eyes and met hers. "But that's why I have to protect Laura. I can't allow her to take the chances her mother and I took growing up. That's why I don't want her to be influenced by you."

Gracie gasped and took a step back. She turned and fled from the house as disillusionment and horrible pain tore her apart inside.

Will sat stunned for a moment at the words that had come out of his mouth. Had he really accused Gracie of being a danger to Laura? The front door opened and closed with a dull thud, breaking him out of his stupor. He bolted from the chair and raced for the door. He jerked it open in time to see Gracie walking swiftly across the area between the house and the tree. What an idiot he'd been. "Gracie! Please, wait."

She didn't slow, but her long skirts kept her from running, even though she'd gathered the hem in one hand and held the fabric a few inches above her ankles.

Will cleared the porch in one bound and extended his stride into a full run as he hit the packed dirt. Within a dozen strides he'd caught her. "Gracie, let me explain. I'm sorry." He touched her shoulder but didn't grasp it.

She slowed then stopped, but kept her back turned to him. "There's nothing to explain. I see now why you don't want me around Laura. Don't worry, I'll stay away."

"No, that's not it. I didn't mean to make you feel that way. I was trying to explain why I don't want her climbing trees or doing things where she might get hurt. She doesn't understand, but I was hoping you might."

Gracie pivoted and looked at him. "I do understand. I accept your apology and I'm saddened by your story, but I believe you truly think I'm a bad influence, or the words wouldn't have come out of your mouth."

Will wished he could wipe the anguish off her face— wished he could wrap his arms around her and pull her close—but he had no right. "Let me prove it to you. Go on a picnic with Laura and me tomorrow. Come over in the morning, and we'll do chores for Deborah and Curt, help with the children and fix the family a nice noon meal. Then we can pack something for the three of us and let them rest. How does that sound? We could go to the pond nearby, and Laura can take a fishing pole. She's been badgering me to teach her to fish, and I'm guessing you're good at that." He cocked his head to the side. "Forgiven?"

She bit her lip and simply watched him for several long seconds. She nodded. "All right." An impish grin softened her face. "And I'll beat you at catching fish any day of the week." She sobered. "But just because I'm agreeing to go, it doesn't mean I believe you're right in being so protective—or that you've shed all thoughts of my bad influence. Don't worry, I'll keep my distance and won't do anything that endangers your niece."

Will's spirits sank. When he'd seen Gracie's sparkling smile peek out, he'd hoped she'd understood his explanation and completely forgiven him, if not moved to a place where she might entertain thoughts of being friends—or even something more.

He couldn't blame her for holding back—every time she'd softened toward him, it seemed he'd said something to push her away. Of course, he'd been burned by Lucinda's deceit and that had made him more cautious, but he refused to entertain that thought. Gracie appeared so much more honest and down to earth than Lucinda. She certainly wouldn't break her word or chase off after another man once she'd come to an understanding.

But doubt niggled at him just the same. How well did he know Gracie Addison, after all?

Gracie helped Will with Deborah's chores the next day and wrestled with whether she should have agreed to go fishing. Deborah was better, but the children had developed runny noses and continued to fuss.

Thankfully, Curt had agreed to finish in the workshop early and take over their late-afternoon and evening care, so Will could take Laura fishing. Will protested, and suggested that he help in the workshop for the morning, but Curt had assured him he was doing more good at the moment helping Gracie, as he had no pressing projects. Gracie narrowed her eyes when she heard his offer to Curt. Was he simply trying to help his boss, or had he already regretted his invitation for her to accompany him and Laura?

She cleared her throat to catch Curt's attention. When he looked up, she gave him a steady look. "Maybe I should stay and help. The twins might be too much for you later if they don't go down for a nap soon."

"Nonsense." Curt shot a furtive glance at Will. "I can handle things fine. You've done far more already than you should have. Besides, I think Laura would be very disappointed if you don't accompany them. That's all she's been talking about this morning."

Gracie noticed that Will didn't look up at Curt's reply, but Laura tugged at Gracie's sleeve. "Please, Miss Gracie. I want you to come with us. Uncle Will said you're very good at catching fish, and he's not."

Something halfway between a snort and a laugh broke from Will's mouth before he stifled it. "That's not exactly what I said, Laura, but I would like Miss Gracie to come, as well." He arched a brow at her. "You haven't changed your mind, I hope? I borrowed two poles, as I thought we could take turns fishing and helping Laura. We might even bring back a string for supper tonight."

Gracie's tension eased as she looked into his hopeful eyes. "Trout for supper sounds good, and I'd hate to disappoint Laura, if Curt is sure he doesn't need my help."

Curt plucked one of the toddlers into his arms as the little boy made his way into the room and headed toward the hot stove. "I'll put them down for a nap as soon as you leave, and then I'll go sit with Deborah. Her eyes have been tired, and she was wishing I could read to her, so the quiet time together will be nice."

Thirty minutes later Gracie spread her skirt and settled onto a blanket covering a small portion of the grassy bank close to the pond. She loved the setting, although she would have liked it to be a little farther from the main road into town. But the pond was right on the border of Curt and Deborah's farm, so they easily walked the short distance.

Will glanced at the spot beside her with a longing look but ushered Laura to the edge of the pond instead. The next few minutes were spent baiting her hook with a wiggling worm, which made the girl squeal, but she got excited when he cast the line into the water and handed her the pole. "Hold it quiet now. Wait until you feel a tug before you try to bring the fish in."

She nodded, her face aglow, and gripped the bamboo rod with both hands. "Is Miss Gracie going to fish?"

Will glanced at Gracie, brows raised.

"Yes, I am. But let's see if you catch anything first. I want you to have the chance to get the biggest fish in the pond if you can."

Laura beamed and turned her attention back to the water.

Gracie's heart swelled with tenderness at Laura's excitement, and at the gentle way Will helped and encouraged the girl. He was so different from what she'd thought after he'd practically yanked her out of the dogwood tree.

She smiled at the memory. Hopefully he'd noticed a bit of difference in her, as well. Somehow she hadn't had the urge to climb a tree since meeting this man.

The clop of hooves on the hard-packed road drew her attention. She swiveled and raised her hand against the bright sun. Her best friend, Carissa Sanderson, drew her mare to a halt along the edge of the road and waved a gloved hand. "Gracie! How nice to see you here." Her gaze moved to Will and then on to Laura. Was that a spark of interest Gracie saw? Her heart contracted. She didn't want to hurt or disappoint her friend if Carissa was interested in Will, but the thought sent a shaft of pain into Gracie's chest.

Carissa's violet skirt cascaded over the seat, and her dark curls were covered by a trim and stylish hat. Her olive skin hinted at being sun-kissed, but Gracie knew it was her mother's Italian blood that gave her such an exotic appearance. She was every bit the lady, in dress, manner, and deportment—something Gracie had given up trying to compete with long ago.

Carissa was one person who never made her feel inferior or less of a woman for being a tomboy, but all of a sudden, Gracie realized how she must look in a man's eyes. Her quickly braided red-gold hair, plain calico dress, and boots, stood in stark contrast to Carissa's striking beauty. How could Will even consider looking at her when someone like Carissa was around?

Chapter 6

Will rose to his feet and bowed to the elegant young woman in the buggy, wondering yet again why he felt no attraction to someone so lovely. The feisty redhead on the blanket at his feet might be the reason, but he still wasn't certain that allowing his heart to get entangled with Gracie was the best idea, no matter how much the idea appealed. "Did you need to talk to me, Miss Sanderson?"

She waved him away. "No, Mr. Montgomery. I was visiting one of my students and saw you fishing. It's good to see you, Gracie. What a lovely day to be outside. Laura, have you caught a fish yet?"

Laura grinned. "No, ma'am. But I'm going to catch me a whopper."

"That sounds lovely, Laura." She picked up her reins. "I should be going."

Will glanced at Gracie, wondering why she'd been so silent. From what he'd been told, Miss Sanderson was a friend of hers. Perhaps Gracie thought him rude for not inviting her to stay. "Would you care to join us?"

He sensed Gracie stiffen and wondered. Had he waited too long to make the invitation? "I'm sure Laura and Miss Addison would enjoy your company."

Gracie nodded but kept silent.

Miss Sanderson shook her head. "I really must be going, but thank you. Gracie, we need to get together sometime soon, now that school is out." She lifted a hand and waved then clucked to her horse and drove down the road.

Gracie pushed to her feet and walked over to Laura's side. "Any nibbles yet?"

"Nope. But a big one is going to bite, I just know it."

Gracie stroked Laura's hair. "Want me to fish with you?"

Laura cocked her head to the side. "If you want to, but I want to catch the first fish. Is that all right?"

Will moved up beside Gracie and tried not to laugh. "The fish will bite whichever worm they want to, Laura. So maybe Gracie and I won't put a line in until you catch your first one." He shot a quick look at Gracie, hoping she'd understand.

She nodded. "That makes perfect sense. Are you hungry yet, Laura?"

"I'm going to eat the fish I catch, so you and Uncle Will can eat the lunch you brought. You can save me some cookies, though." Laura wiggled the tip of the pole and scowled. "Come get the worm, you silly fish."

Will rolled his eyes at Gracie, and she grinned. "Come on, let's dive into that food. Laura might not be hungry, but I certainly am." He held out his hand to Gracie, hoping she could somehow see into his heart.

She hesitated then slipped her fingers into his. Will gave a gentle squeeze. He led her forward to the blanket and seated her. As much as he'd love to continue to hold her hand, it wasn't proper, and she probably wouldn't allow it, but his soul did a little dance that she hadn't totally rejected his gesture.

Gracie tucked the remains of the food into the basket and placed the checkered cloth over the top. If she didn't know better, she'd think her fingers were still tingling from the touch of Will's hand. Strong yet gentle—firm yet tender. She almost hadn't slipped her fingers into his, but something in his eyes had convinced her that he wasn't playing a game.

But where did Carissa fit into this picture—or did she? Gracie had thought she'd seen interest in Will's gaze as he'd looked her direction, and he *had* invited her to stay. Then why be so tender toward her a short time later? None of it made sense—and she was still struggling with his attitude toward her in regard to his niece. They'd had a wonderful visit while eating, but it was all too confusing, and her own growing attraction toward the man certainly didn't help.

Laura plunked down on the blanket and tossed her pole on the grass. "I didn't catch a thing. Dumb fish."

Will squatted next to her. "Keep a good attitude, Laura. Fishing is about having fun as well as catching fish. Maybe next time you'll do better."

"Next time I'm going to swing on that rope over the pond that's hanging from that tree." She pointed along the bank a ways.

Will shaded his eyes and looked then turned his attention to Laura. "No you aren't, young lady. I don't want you going near that tree, do you understand?"

She glowered then pivoted toward Gracie. "You'll help me do it, won't you, Miss Gracie? You wouldn't be afraid of an old rope swing, huh."

Gracie wanted to groan. Right when she felt she'd started earning Will's trust, Laura had to bring up something that upset him. "You must obey your uncle, Laura. It doesn't matter what I've done or might enjoy. Besides, I'm not climbing trees or swinging off ropes anymore. I'm too old for that kind of behavior now." She desperately wanted to see how Will reacted to her statement, but she kept her gaze fixed on Laura.

The little girl crossed her arms. "Huh. You weren't too

old for it a few days ago when you were in that tree."

Gracie's cheeks heated. "I was being foolish. I won't be doing it again. Regardless, you listen to what your uncle tells you, all right?"

Will held out his hands to both Laura and Gracie. "Come on, let me help you ladies up, and we'll head home. Then I'd like to drive you back to your house, if you'll allow me to, Gracie."

His hand touched hers, and a jolt of awareness raced through her. Gracie was certain her cheeks flamed as bright as her hair, but she nodded. "Thank you. It *has* been a long day, and walking home doesn't sound too appealing." She detected a flicker of something that looked like disappointment in his eyes.

Had he hoped she might throw herself at him in gratitude for the ride? She liked Will Montgomery, but she couldn't possibly be in love with him. Besides, she didn't care to give him the wrong impression—no matter how warm or tingly she got when he touched her or how much she ached to have it continue.

Will took Gracie's arm and helped her into Curt's buggy. He still wasn't sure what to make of this woman. He'd thought she was interested in him after the time they'd spent together working side by side in Deborah and Curt's home and then on the picnic beside the pond. She'd been less than enthusiastic in her acceptance of his offer to take her home when he was hoping she'd see it as the first step toward something more serious. Maybe he should declare his interest, but would she reject him the way Lucinda had done?

And then there was Laura. Even though Gracie said she'd given up her tomboy ways, it had only been a matter of days since she'd proven otherwise. Did he want a sweetheart who might be a poor influence on his niece—even to the point of her getting hurt? He ran his hands over his hair then picked up the reins and shook them. "Get on, Charlie."

Gracie swayed on the seat beside him as the wheels went into a rut, her shoulder touching his. She gripped the handrail beside her. "I'm sorry for jostling you. Is everything all right? You've been very quiet since we left the house."

He pulled himself out of his musing, annoyed that he'd not saved his thoughts for later. As much as he worried about Laura, he couldn't deny the growing attraction he felt for this delightful young woman beside him. "Everything is fine. I enjoyed our time together today, and I think Laura did, as well."

"So did I. She's a precocious child with a strong spirit, but she's also refreshing and delightful."

A warm glow suffused Will at the compliment. "Thank you. If I can only keep her safe as she grows up, I'll be grateful and feel I've done my job as her guardian." He turned toward her and grinned. "But she can be a handful, I'll freely admit that."

They passed the next few minutes until they reached Gracie's home in comfortable conversation. Will drew up at the front gate, set the brake, and jumped down. He walked around to Gracie's side to help her, and the front door opened.

A young man stood there. He walked to the edge of the porch and lifted a hand in greeting, but a frown gave him a decidedly sour appearance. "Gracie. I've come to take you to supper at the restaurant. Your father told me you were to be home by now. You have kept me waiting for over half an hour."

Will stared at the man. Clean shaven, dressed in a finer suit than Will could afford, and holding a top hat that would typically be seen in a city. All in all, the man was a dandy, and a supercilious one at that. "I apologize for making Miss Addison late for her appointment."

He reached up and helped Gracie down without meeting her eyes. She appeared struck dumb by the man, although she made choking noises and kept a tight grip on his arm.

"I hope you have a fine evening with your beau, Miss Addison." He vaulted into the seat and slapped the horse with the reins, sending the animal into a startled trot.

Chapter 7

Gracie found her voice and let out a startled cry of dismay as Will's buggy disappeared around a corner. How dare Jerold show up at her door and act as though they had an understanding. She hadn't agreed to go anywhere with this man, nor would she. Ever. She hiked up her skirt and almost bolted after the buggy.

She halted. She'd never catch it at the rate it was moving. "What is the meaning of this?" She pivoted slowly to glare at Jerold. "Why did you imply that we had an agreement to meet for supper?" She grabbed the gate and swung it open then stalked toward the porch.

Jerold hunched one shoulder without seeming to notice her distress. "Your father told me you'd be home soon, and since I was unable to come the evening you invited me, I thought I'd make it up to you now."

"Did my father suggest this?"

He hesitated a moment. "Well, not exactly." The corners of his mouth ticked up. "But I'm sure he'd approve."

She shook her head. "I'm truly sorry, Jerold. You're a nice man, but I'm not interested. Please forgive me, but I'm going up to my room."

He drew back as though she'd slapped him. "I'd think, at your age, you'd be happy to have a suitor." His shock dropped away, and a superior smile took its place. "Especially one who can point you down the right path for your life."

Gracie gave a mocking laugh. "You make nineteen—almost twenty—years of age sound like quite a spinster. And believe me when I tell you that I know exactly where my path lies and how I intend to get there—and it is not with you." She flounced past him, yanked open the door, and hurried inside. She slammed the door behind her.

"Father? Papa? Are you home?" She was thankful he hadn't suggested this meeting, but he'd probably hoped she'd be too polite to spurn Jerold's advances. He might have even hoped she'd accompany the man to supper and fall for his charms, if he had any.

She stomped up the stairs to her room and threw herself on the bed. What about Will? He'd gotten the wrong idea from Jerold and thought the man was her beau. She shivered at the thought of the life she'd have if she married Jerold. How arrogant to assume she'd be thrilled at his company and to think she couldn't attract anyone else.

Gracie tucked a pillow behind her shoulders. What should she do about Will? Should she ask him what he thought of Carissa then ease into her opinion of Jerold? No, that would be forward and would give away her concern that he might be interested in her best friend. What then?

She rolled over and punched the pillow, hating the situation she found herself in. Will had sparked more interest in her than any man she'd ever met, and she had just started to think he might find her intriguing, as well. Now this.

Something her father had often said came back full force. *"When in doubt, pray."* He had a solid faith that God loved us no matter what the circumstances might show. But he also said that our emotions aren't a good test of whether God is at work in our lives or not—only the Bible and prayer could show us the truth.

She plucked the Bible off her nightstand and settled into her pillows once more. "Father, show me Your truth. Give me Your wisdom." She flipped the pages and started to read, assured that her heavenly Father had heard, just as her earthly father had promised.

Five days dragged by without Will getting so much as a glimpse of Gracie. She hadn't shown up at Curt and Deborah's on Sunday, the day after their picnic, and he started to work the following day. He should have gone to services with Curt and Deborah, but now that she was feeling a little better, Will offered to watch the children so the couple could attend on their own. Both of the toddlers were still fighting sniffles, and their parents were concerned about taking them out.

Will had wanted to go, certain that Gracie would be there, but he'd also hated the thought of seeing her sitting with that man who'd waited at her house. From what the man had said, he could only surmise they were headed toward courtship, and he'd rather not watch it play out.

He enjoyed his job in Curt's shop, but he had a hard time keeping his mind on some of the more intricate details.

Curt walked in as Will gazed out the window toward town. "Something bothering you, Will?"

He jumped like a jackrabbit spooked by a hawk. "I'm sorry. I guess I was gathering wool. It won't happen again."

Curt nodded, but he didn't seem convinced. "Thanks for all the help you've been in the house. That's not what I hired you for, but I'll admit it came at the right time."

Will relaxed at the change in subject, happy Curt hadn't pushed to find out what might be wrong. "Glad to.

You and Deborah didn't have to take me and Laura in. You could have insisted we find our own place. I'll be doing that soon, of course, but it's been a blessing to get my feet under me first."

The brisk sound of footfalls in the office leading to the workroom turned Will and Curt around. Will moved forward. "Want me to see who it is?"

Curt shook his head. "I've been expecting a customer. You go ahead and keep working on this headboard. Mrs. Williams is anxious to get it next week, and it still needs sanding and another coat of varnish." He strode across the room then stepped through the open door into the small office area tucked into a corner of the building.

Will reached for the sanding block, thankful he didn't have to concentrate on anything more detailed.

"Uncle Will?" Laura's breathless voice took him by surprise, and he jerked his head up.

"Where did you come from, pumpkin?"

She grinned. "Pumpkins are for pie, silly. May I go fishing?"

"Maybe later, when I get off work."

She bounced from one foot to the other. "How about wading in the edge of the pond? Can I do that alone? Please? You'll be working all day, and I'm hot and bored."

He set his brush down. "Not without an adult."

"Miss Gracie is here. May I go if she'll take me?"

"Here? Where?" He stepped to the window and peered

out toward the house, his heart picking up its pace.

"She's visiting Miss Deborah and the babies."

"Did she come alone?"

Laura scrunched up her face. "Yes. She always comes alone, doesn't she?"

He shrugged, feeling foolish that his first thought was of the arrogant man who'd been on Gracie's porch. "I don't want you to bother Miss Gracie while she's visiting. I told you I'd take you later. All right?"

She gave him a mutinous look that he couldn't quite decipher, then slowly nodded. "Yes, sir. I won't bother her while she's visiting." She swung around and marched out the door without looking back.

Over an hour passed, but Gracie didn't go home and Curt didn't return—nor did Laura come back to pester him. A feeling of niggling doubt tore at him. Would Laura disobey him and ask Gracie to take her fishing?

He set the sanding block aside and wiped his hands on a rag. He'd clean up later. Right now he'd better check on his niece.

Gracie stood with hands planted on her hips, wishing she'd checked with Will first, but she'd hated to trouble him at work—and she'd dreaded seeing accusation in his eyes after what happened last week. She took a step closer to Laura, where the girl waded ankle deep in the water. "Are you certain your uncle said you could come?"

Laura raised innocent eyes. "He said I could if I had a big person with me. That's why I came and asked you. I knew Miss Deborah wouldn't want to leave the children, with them coming down sick, and you're so nice." She dimpled and walked out a little deeper into the pond, the water covering her ankles as she lifted the hem of her short skirt. "I'm having lots of fun. May I go deeper and get all wet? It's hot today, and it would feel awfully good."

Gracie hesitated. Should she take Laura back and ask Will to be certain? The child was already here, so maybe a few minutes of fun wouldn't hurt. After all, Will kept Laura on such a tight rein that she felt sorry for the girl. "I suppose you can sit down there, but no deeper. Understood?"

Laura nodded. "I'll be good." She sank into the water, which only came up a few inches.

Gracie sighed. "I'm going to sit against that tree and rest for a minute. I'll still be able to see you, but I'm holding you to your promise to be good." She traipsed to the tree a few yards away and sank down on the grass at the base of the trunk then leaned her head against it and closed her eyes for a few seconds. She thought she heard something and looked toward Laura, but the child was still playing in the same spot, leaning forward and dribbling handfuls of water over her bare toes. She didn't have a swimsuit, so she'd worn an old dress that was too short for her, and removed her stockings and shoes.

Gracie shut her eyes again. It felt good after so little sleep the last few nights, worrying about Will and what he might think. This was ridiculous. She needed to simply tell him she had no interest in Jerold. She opened her eyes again to check on Laura and gasped. The girl wasn't in her place at the edge of the pond. She'd closed her eyes for ten seconds, if that. Gracie jumped to her feet and dashed toward the water. "Laura? Where are you? Answer me this instant!"

"I'm up here. Look at how good I climbed this tree, Miss Gracie, just like you! Now I'm going to swing on this rope. I'm a daredevil, too. Aren't you proud of me?" Laura stood on a low branch in a nearby maple, clutching a rope suspended from a higher branch.

Gracie sucked in a breath, her hand going to her mouth. She dashed for the tree. "No!" If she could get there before Laura swung out over the water—

Something crashed through the brush not far behind her, but Gracie didn't take time to look. "Laura. Get down before you get hurt!" Gracie felt as though she hollered the words, but they seemed to come out on a whisper instead.

Laura squealed in glee and pushed off from the branch, gripping the rope. She swung out over the pond. The rope reached the full arc and stopped then slowly began to return. Laura's shouts of delight suddenly turned to a cry of alarm. "My hands are slipping! I can't hold on!"

She shrieked again as her grip loosened, and she fell into the water. Gracie watched in horror as the child disappeared. She tore at the buttons holding her skirts. She was a good swimmer—surely she could reach Laura and bring her back to the surface.

Chapter 8

Will shot past Gracie, his feet thundering against the sod. "Laura, I'm almost there."

Laura's head popped to the surface just as Will plunged into the pond. In three hard strides through the deepening water, he'd reached Laura's side and plucked her into his arms. She coughed and spluttered, but she didn't appear any worse for her adventure. He hugged her tight against his chest and waded toward the shore. When he got there, he set Laura on the grassy bank and knelt in front of her, shaking with fear. "First, are you all right?"

"Uh-huh." She nodded, her streaming hair hanging loose around her face. "That was fun. And when you picked me up, my feet touched the bottom. Can I do it again, Uncle Will?"

His fear dissolved into anger, and it was all he could do not to shake the little imp. "What were you thinking coming here? I said I'd take you after work."

She shook her head. "Nuh-uh. You said I couldn't come without a big person, so I asked Miss Gracie, and she said she'd come. So I didn't disobey you."

He ground his teeth in frustration at the child's reasoning. "You could have drowned, or hit your head on a rock, or fallen out of that tree and been killed. Besides, I told you not to bother Miss Gracie. Remember that?"

She tilted her head to the side. "Yes, but I didn't ask her until she was done visiting with Mrs. Warren. I didn't mean to be bad. I was so hot and sticky, and I wanted to play in the water. And it was fun! You should try it."

He groaned then reached down and wrung out her skirt. "Go sit on the grass up by that tree where Miss Gracie was earlier. I need to talk to her alone. And do not move until I get there, or you'll go without supper."

Laura stuck out her lower lip, but she obeyed, trudging up the gently sloping bank to the tree.

He rounded on Gracie who stood clasping her hands in a tight grip, her entire body shaking. Pity engulfed him, but he pushed it away as the memory of the little girl going under the water returned. "I asked Laura, but I'll ask you, as well. What were you thinking, allowing her to climb a tree and swing out over that water? Couldn't you see it was dangerous?"

Gracie's stomach roiled, and she thought she might be sick. She didn't blame Will for being angry. This was her fault. No matter what Laura had said, she should have checked with Will. "I'm so sorry. She said it was all right with you, but I should have asked."

"That isn't what I'm upset about. I know Laura can be very persuasive. But why did you allow her in that tree when you know how I feel about it? And to let her swing on that rope—" He closed his eyes for a brief moment.

"I'd checked on her a couple of times, and she was just sitting in a few inches of water nearby. She promised she'd be good. I only closed my eyes for a few seconds. I don't see how she could have gotten to the tree and climbed it in that amount of time." She placed her fingertips over her lips to stifle a sob. "She was my responsibility. I was wrong to not keep my eyes on her every second."

He gave a curt nod. "And from what I heard her say before she swung over the pond, she was mimicking you. There's only one thing I can do so this never happens again. I'll have to ask you to stay away from Laura." He pivoted and stalked toward the little girl sitting quietly under the tree.

Gracie wanted to sink to the ground and cry, but she stood erect, holding her head high. She'd been remiss in closing her eyes for those few seconds, but it wasn't her fault Laura hadn't obeyed Will, nor was it her responsibility that the girl wanted to be like her. So be it. If he didn't want her to see Laura again, she wouldn't see him, either. She plucked up her skirts and headed for home. She was done with this man, no matter how much the decision hurt.

Will didn't look back as he gripped Laura's hand and led her across the meadow toward the Warren home. His anger was fading, and sadness took its place. He was thankful his niece was safe, but had he been completely fair in placing the blame on Gracie? Laura could be very persuasive and was prone to disobey. Had Gracie really done anything so wrong? It hurt his heart to even think about not seeing her again.

"Uncle Will, you're holding my hand too tight." Laura tugged at him.

"I'm not letting go of you until we reach the house. You're to go straight to your room, change your clothes, and lie down until supper. With no arguments, young lady."

She gave a huge sigh. "Yes, sir. But you were mean to Miss Gracie. It wasn't her fault I went on the swing. I sneaked up there when her eyes were shut."

He ignored her as he battled his own conscience. They arrived at the house, and he waited until Laura scurried up the steps to her room, then he made his way back to the workshop.

Curt stood in the doorway, his eyes filled with concern. "Where's Gracie? And why is Laura dripping wet?"

Will waved him back inside and sank into a chair. "It's not a pretty story, but if you have a few minutes. . ."

Curt nodded and took a seat. "I have all the time you need."

Over the next few minutes, Will poured out the story, including his history and the loss of his sister. All the pain and guilt spewed out in a jumble of words that he couldn't seem to stem. Finally, he wiped his hand across his sweaty brow and gave a feeble smile. "Probably way more than you cared to hear, but I'll admit, it feels good to get it off my chest."

"I imagine it does. I'm sorry to hear about Laura's mother. I understand now why you're so protective of Laura."

Something in Curt's tone caught Will's attention, and he lifted his head. "You think I'm *too* protective."

Curt gave a half shrug. "It's not my concern. You're her uncle, not me."

Will tensed. "I want to know what you think."

Curt hesitated. "All right." He gave a short nod. "I

believe your guilt over your sister's death has influenced you more than you realize."

"How so?" Will wasn't sure he wanted to hear this, but somehow he knew he needed to listen. He'd been praying long and hard lately that he'd make wise decisions where Laura, and even Gracie, was concerned, and after the past hour, he was second-guessing everything he'd done and said.

Curt leaned forward, his hands on his knees, and met Will's gaze. "Let's take my children as an example. They're sick right now and even have a low fever. I could race to the doctor—worry over them until I make myself sick with fear. Or, I can choose to trust God with my twins, knowing He loves them more than I do. Of course, if they get worse, I'll be sensible and call the doctor. But their health and the length of their lives is ultimately God's decision, not mine, no matter how much I try to protect them."

"So you think I'm wrong to protect Laura?" Frustration put a sharp edge to his question, and Will tried to soften it. "I don't want something to happen to her like it did to her mother."

"But your guilt over the belief that you caused your sister's death is what fuels that desire." He held up his hands. "I'm not saying you don't love your niece. I'm saying it's not normal to force a little girl with a sense of adventure to never climb a tree or swing on a rope or anything else that might contain a hint of danger."

Will leaned back and crossed his arms. "So you would have let her go on that rope swing? Even if she could have drowned?"

"Did you pay attention to how deep it was where she landed? I've been on that swing, and at the deepest point where you could let go, the water comes up to my neck, and Laura isn't heavy enough to have swung that far. There's not a rock on the bottom of that pond that I've ever found.

"Should she have done it without proper supervision? Of course not. Should she be denied ever having new experiences that other children have? I don't think so. And certainly not to satisfy your sense of guilt over an event that probably would have happened, regardless."

Will winced as he tried to take in all that Curt said. He bowed his head and pondered. "And Gracie?" He finally raised his head. "How about her part in this?"

Curt arched one brow. "I think you're falling in love with her and don't want to admit it, out of fear that Laura will want to be like her. Gracie Addison is a fine young woman, and one I'd be happy to have my daughter emulate when she gets older. She shouldn't have closed her eyes for those few seconds, but are you going to blame her for that forever and cut off any chance of happiness for both of you?"

Curt shook his head when Will stayed silent. "It

doesn't sound sensible to me." He slapped his hands on his knees and stood. "I'm going to check on Deborah and the children. The afternoon is pretty much gone. Go see to your niece." He gave Will a sly look. "And anything else that might need to be taken care of, before it's too late."

Gracie had never been much of a crier, but right now she wanted to beat on her pillow and wail the loss of Laura and Will. Especially Will. When had she allowed the man to burrow himself so deeply into her heart? Jerold Carnegie might be boring, but at least marrying him wouldn't have brought this kind of pain. She snorted. No, but she'd warrant she'd have another whole set of problems to deal with, married to that man.

She was thankful her father was at work when she got home, so she'd been able to slip into her room without being seen—or questioned. Papa knew she'd been helping Deborah and Curt, and he'd started questioning her lately about the new man working there. Her blushes had given him all the information he'd needed, and he'd informed her he intended to meet Will and see if he passed muster. She'd cringed at the thought, but now it didn't matter. Will didn't care to see her again.

A knock at the door reverberated through the house, then it came again. She swung her legs over the edge of the bed and pushed to her feet. If it was Jerold, she'd send him packing with no doubt to her feelings this time. She was in no mood to be trifled with after losing Will and Laura.

Gracie threw open the door, her lips wide to get in the first word before Jerold could speak, but they closed as soon as she saw Will, hat in his hands. Stunned, she stood with her heart thudding a dull beat in her ears.

He gestured toward the parlor through the open door. "May I come in and speak to you?"

She nodded and stepped aside. Papa would be home any moment, and they probably should sit on the porch until he arrived, but right now she didn't care about propriety. She simply wanted to get this over—there was nothing romantic about his request. Will had come to make sure she'd understood his demand at the pond about Laura.

"Would you care for coffee?"

"No, thank you. May I sit?" He stood uneasily before an overstuffed chair.

"Please." She perched on one across the room. "I know why you're here, and I'll honor your request not to see Laura again."

He bolted from the chair and stood, towering over her. "That's not why I'm here." He clutched his hat so hard the brim crinkled. "I owe you an apology, Gracie."

"What?" She met his gaze for the first time. "No, you don't."

"Yes. I was harsh to you at the pond, and I had no right." He sucked in a sharp breath and plunged on. "Curt gave me a good talking to when I got back, and he's right. I've been letting guilt over my sister's death color everything I do with Laura—and with how I've been treating you."

She listened, not sure she understood. "Could you explain, please?"

He nodded and settled onto the edge of the sofa nearby, only an arm's length from her. "You are so similar to my sister that it scared me. The same bright, sunny personality—the same sense of adventure and fun. You've been trying to disguise it these past few days, I think maybe to show me you aren't a danger to Laura, but it's who you are.

"Part of me has been worried for Laura, but I realized today that the other part has been terrified to allow myself to fall in love with you, on the chance you might get hurt. Or worse, do something foolish and die. I couldn't face that possibility, so I pushed you away."

Gracie sat still, trying to take it all in. Only one thing he'd said stood out. "Terrified to allow yourself to fall in love with me? Is that what you said?" Joy tried to sing through her heart, but fear that she'd heard wrong tamped it back down.

He nodded then reached out his hand and clasped hers. "I know it's too soon to say this—we haven't known each other long—but I care for you, Gracie, more than I've ever cared for any woman. I want a chance to get to know you better. To court you as a woman like you deserves to be courted and, I hope, win your love in return." He paused and sucked in another breath. "That is, unless that fellow who was here the other day has beat me to it."

She giggled and shook her head. "Jerold Carnegie? I think not. I sent him packing a few minutes after you left. I had nothing to do with him appearing on my doorstep, nor did I care to have him stay." She sobered as another thought smote her. "But what about Carissa?"

"Who?" His face was a total blank.

Gracie relaxed. "Miss Sanderson, Laura's teacher. I thought you might be interested in her."

His eyes widened. "She's a very nice lady, but she seems a bit tame. Definitely nothing like a fiery redhead I know." He raised the back of her hand to his lips and pressed a kiss there, long and slow. "Would you allow me to court you, Gracie? With the hope that one day I might win you as my bride?"

A step sounded in the open doorway and Gracie looked up. Her father stood there, a bemused look on his face. "So what do you have to say to this young man's question, my girl? I've been talking to Curt Warren about Will, and it seems he's a good worker and an honest man." He turned his attention to Will. "And while I'd have preferred he ask my permission to court you first, I'll allow it if it's what you want."

Will pushed to his feet and drew Gracie with him, nodding his thanks to her father. He waited, both of her hands held in his.

She raised her face and smiled. "I'd like that very much. I've known since the day you pulled me out of that tree and I landed in your lap that I cared for you." Warmth flowed into her cheeks, but she kept her gaze steady on his. "I'm a bit forward, but you'll have to take me as I am. Although I'll promise not to climb any more trees if that makes you happy."

Will drew Gracie closer. "I don't care how many trees you climb, or teach Laura to climb. I'll even build you both a tree house if you'd like that. I've decided to trust both of you to God's loving care and quit worrying. As long as you'll be careful and promise me one thing."

Her heart skittering like a filly bounding through a meadow in the springtime, she nodded. "Anything."

"I know I said we'd court, but since you said you care, I hope you won't make me wait too long." He leaned down and pressed a tender kiss to her lips. "I'm praying you'll consider becoming my summertime bride—that you might marry me in a couple months, before fall sets in, under the dogwood tree where we first met. There's nothing that would make me happier."

Gracie looked at her father and saw his happy

expression. She laid her cheek against Will's chest to feel his own racing heartbeat and sighed. "Nor me. A summertime bride sounds about as perfect as anything can be."

Miralee Ferrell and her husband, Allen, live on eleven acres in Washington State. Miralee loves interacting with people, ministering at her church, (she is a certified lay counselor with the AACC), riding her horse, and playing with her dogs. An award-winning and bestselling author, she speaks at various women's functions and has taught at writers' conferences. Since 2007, she's had ten books released, both in women's contemporary fiction and historical romance. Miralee recently started a newsletter, and you can sign up for it on her website/blog at www.miraleeferrell.com.

THE COLUMBINE BRIDE

BRIDE

Davalynn Spencer

Thou wilt shew me the path of life.
PSALM 16:11

Chapter 1

Colorado, 1886

Lucy Powell's ears pricked at her children's excited voices. She looked up from the vegetable seed packets to the candy counter where a tall bearded man reached for Elmore's ear. Three quick steps took her past a table before she stopped. The man squatted, and her son's eyes widened at the sight of a copper penny. Cecilia, ever the guardian, stayed her little brother's hand.

"We don't take things from strangers, Elmore."

Lucy clutched the packets she'd already chosen and listened for her son's reply.

"He ain't no stranger, Sissy. That penny come out of my ear."

Cecilia pulled him back with a sharp whisper, eyes narrowed at the man. "It's just a trick. He fooled you."

Elmore's lower lip bulged, and Lucy suppressed an impulse to intervene. Intrigued by her daughter's protective instincts and partially hidden by a display of granite ironware, she inched forward, waiting to see if Cecilia had the pluck she suspected.

"Pardon me saying so, miss, but you've got something in your ear, too."

The man's warm voice touched forgotten places in Lucy's mind and weakened her daughter's defenses as well. He reached toward one dark braid, and six-year-old eyes rounded at a second mysterious penny. Lucy covered her mouth and blinked back a burning sensation as he straightened and laid both coins on the counter.

"I'd thank you kindly if you'd help me out with these since I have other things I need to tend to."

Lucy stepped forward. The man set his hat on, turned on his heel, and strode squarely into her.

"Oh!" Seed packets scattered as she flailed for balance. The man's arm linked around her waist, and he jerked his hat off and mashed it against his leg, dangling her from his arm. "Pardon me, ma'am."

Emboldened by her motherly motives and the ragged beard sweeping her forehead, Lucy gathered her footing, pushed out of the man's grasp, and bent to retrieve her potential garden. He joined her, scooping up most of the packets as she scooped up her breath.

"No harm done." She accepted what he'd gathered and

scoured the beard bristling above her before lifting her eyes to meet his. She stilled at their clarity—blue as the sky. And slightly familiar.

"I hope you don't mind them having a sweet." One eye tightened at the corner with an unspoken thought.

She regarded her children, whose hope plastered their faces like a newspaper headline, then returned her attention to the man. "How very kind of you. Thank you."

He nodded and stepped around her toward the hardware. Lucy tried to imagine what he looked like clean shaven. Clutching the seed packets, she joined her children, who were less concerned with her near trampling than with how many licorice whips could be bought for a penny. Cecilia's calculating pleased Lucy, though guilt warred with sensibility as she justified not treating her children to this simple pleasure since their father had died. She did not have money for nonessentials, not with saving everything to buy supplies for the summer. And were it not for Mr. Wellington's generosity at the mercantile, they'd have even less. His tally always came out different than what Lucy calculated. He'd best not let Cecilia help him with the order.

May was spent, school out for summer, and Lucy and the children would leave tomorrow for the ranch to salvage what they could from winter's neglect. *Ranch* seemed such a grand term for their two sections and handful of cows, but it had been William's dream, and Lucy determined not to let it die as well. By now their small herd must be scattered to the hills and their hay field decimated by deer. But she and the children could plow and plant, round up and repair. Rubbing the tightness that lately pulled between her neck and shoulder, she sagged against the counter.

"You all right, Mrs. Powell?" Fred Wellington's squeaky question announced his approach, and she straightened. The man's generous spirit must be what endeared his wife and daughter to him, for Lucy could not imagine living day in and day out with that voice. Though it couldn't be much worse than living with no husband or father's voice at all.

Glancing toward the stranger, she found him looking at coffeepots of all things. Mr. Wellington's daughter, Priscilla, had come from the back and wore lovely flushed cheeks as she presented a varied selection to the man whose voice could melt ice on a winter pond.

"Mrs. Powell?"

"Oh—yes, Mr. Wellington." She stashed her curiosity and opened her reticule. If only the stranger could work his sleight of hand with her meager savings, then she would not be weighing the value of sugar over sorghum molasses and Arbuckles' over tea. Wellington penciled her items on his notepad, tore off the sheet, and slid it across the counter. Lucy read the figure and drew a deep breath. "I don't know what we—"

He raised a palm to interrupt. "Good Lord takes care

of us all, Mrs. Powell. 'Sides, what the Spruce City school board gives you I am sure would not keep a tiger in stripes."

"Fredrick, really." The man's wife swept around the end of the counter and swatted his shoulder with a feathery touch. What a pair they were, one tall and squeaky, the other plump yet elegant. But a pair, two halves of one whole. "It's none of our business what Mrs. Powell receives." Rosemary Wellington's cheeks puffed with a pleasant smile as the children giggled over the sacks her husband handed them with much more than a penny's worth of candy in each.

"Thank you, Mr. Wellington," Cecilia said in her most proper voice.

"Thank you," Elmore parroted.

Rosemary shook her head. "Looks like Mr. Reiter has been at it again."

Reiter. That was it. Buck Reiter, the next rancher over the ridge who ran horses with his widowed sister. Pulling the draw on her reticule, Lucy turned casually toward the hardware and stole another quick glance. The man helped raise his nephew, from what Lucy had heard, though that was years before she and William came to Spruce City. The boy was grown and married now, just last Christmas, if she recalled correctly.

Ducking her head, she fingered the hair knotted at her neck and caught the sweep of her black wool, so dark and hot for the summer's work ahead. Tomorrow she'd pack it away. Cows and coyotes would not notice if she put off her widow's weeds a bit early.

"I'll load your supplies and have you on your way quick as a wink." Wellington hefted a sack of flour on one shoulder and headed out, while his wife shuttled the children through the door to wait on the boardwalk. Then she turned to Lucy.

"I am so glad you're not leaving us, dear, but do you have anyone to help you? There are several strapping boys here in town who could lend a hand."

Indeed there were, but with what would Lucy pay them? Free spelling and arithmetic lessons they'd left behind for the summer? She smiled at Rosemary's kindness. "I want to see what needs doing first. Maybe then I'll have someone help me find the cattle and build up the woodpile."

Lucy shivered, but not with cold. The woodpile had indirectly led to William's death when rogue lightning struck the tree he was cutting. A throat cleared and she looked up to see Mr. Reiter crumpling his hat in his hands again. She squelched the urge to slap his fingers.

"We've wood for three winters at our place, ma'am. I'd be happy to bring over a wagonload."

The man confessed to eavesdropping, yet showed not one shred of embarrassment. She pulled the cord of her already tightened reticule and looked out the storefront windows. "Thank you, but that won't be necessary. We will be fine." Accepting Mr. Wellington's deliberately poor ciphering skills was one thing, but taking charity from a neighbor she could never repay was quite another.

His retreating boots pricked her pride. A part of her wouldn't mind seeing the deep-voiced Buck Reiter drive into their yard with a wagonload of wood. But a bigger part feared letting anyone see how bad things really were.

Chapter 2

Liquid they were, and warm, like hot syrup on biscuits. The widow Powell's dark eyes sent a shiver up Buck's spine in spite of the sweat collecting at his hatband. She had scrutinized his beard as if it held clues to his breakfast, and he pulled his fingers through it, hearing again his sister's scolding to shave.

Picking up a Gem Food Chopper he didn't need, he nodded at Priscilla Wellington's prattle about the ease of grinding vegetables and meat. Wouldn't he be a dandy with a food mill in his saddlebags, breaking trail through the mountains on the hunt for high pasture—which reminded him why he was in the mercantile to begin with. He'd volunteered to pick up Lilly's supplies so he could lay in his own provisions without causing a stir. He didn't need much, just some ground coffee and dried beef. Beans, salt pork, canned fruit. Come to think of it, he needed a plate and cup, too. Lilly would fuss and fret and try to make him stay, but it was time. He had a string of mares and a fine yearling colt comin' on as his share of the ranch. If his sister looked straight at the situation, she'd see that twelve years were enough. She and her boy had moved on with their lives. It was time he did the same.

He huffed and cranked the chopper's wooden handle. The widow had turned him down flat. Fool woman. Did she expect to chop her own wood and do all the chores herself with two young'uns? He cut a look her way, and like a queen she bid Wellington's wife good-bye, walked out to her buckboard, climbed in, and drove away. Again he combed his fingers through his beard.

Two hours later, he drove beneath the high gate where HORNE RANCH hung across the road on a long flat timber. He'd burned the sign himself when he wasn't much more than a colt. A wedding gift for Lilly and her new husband, Nathaniel Horne. Buck never dreamed that a decade later, the ranch would become his home for the next dozen years—years that most men use to find a place of their own and raise a family. But he couldn't leave his big sister and her boy alone in the Rocky Mountains after Nathaniel died. No more than he could turn a deaf ear to what he heard today at Wellington's.

Lucy Powell didn't want his help, but it wasn't in him

to sit by idle when he had what she needed. Besides, his days as substitute father and foreman were near done, and he'd be setting out soon.

When he pulled up at the ranch house, Lilly and Nate's wife, Ara, were wrestling sheets at the line. Ara stopped to press her hands against her arched back, looking like she carried two foals instead of one. Lilly would have his hide if she heard him comparing her daughter-in-law to a mare, but there wasn't that much difference between animals and people when it came to bringing on new ones. Beetle lay in the shade by the open barn door, which meant Nate was inside mucking stalls. A mongrel pup tugged on the dog's ear the same way leaving the ranch tugged on Buck's insides.

He stacked their stores on the wide porch, and Lilly came out the front door with a pitcher and two glasses.

"I don't know what we'd do without you." She handed him a glass and took one of the rockers. He folded into the other and nearly told her exactly what she'd do without him. She'd do just fine.

"Glad to help." He pulled off his hat, sleeved his forehead, and downed half the lemonade. Too early for the evening breeze. Everything but his thoughts stood still and held its breath, waiting for a break in the heat. "You know the widow Powell?"

Lilly slowly nodded and set the rocker to moving. "The new teacher. Lost her husband late last summer when dry lightning sparked a fire. Searchers found him beneath a charred tree, didn't they?"

"That'd be the one." He finished off his glass and reached for the pitcher on the railing. "Saw her at Wellington's today."

Lilly stilled her chair with a toe. "I thought she was leaving, selling out."

He cut his sister a look. "Like you did?"

She eyed him over her glass and pushed damp hair off her forehead. "I never considered leaving, not for one second. Then you showed up." Her weathered hand patted his on the rocker arm and gave a slight squeeze. "Nate and I would not have survived here without you."

An old conversation, played out more times than Buck cared to count. "Good Lord had more to do with it than me." The good Lord would do right by Lucy Powell, too, but somehow Buck wanted to be in on it. "She was laying in stores, and Wellington's wife tried to talk her into hiring help. She's got two babies at her skirt, can't be more than five or six. I figure she doesn't have much money because not much crossed the counter." He downed the last of his drink. "Other than my two cents."

Palming the lemonade from his mustache, he caught Lilly's look, her thoughts as plain as a pencil mark on a tally sheet. "Remember that trick Pa used to pull when we wanted candy?"

Lilly resumed her rocking. "I could never manage it

without dropping the coin. But if I recall, you were quite good. Even fooled Nate a time or two."

He huffed at the memory, a clear reminder of just how long he'd been there. "Gave each young'un a penny and waited around till Wellington loaded her order. From what I could tell, she's set on getting the place in shape by herself. I offered her a load of firewood, but she turned me down flat." Another huff and he shoved his hat on, handed Lilly the glass with his thanks. He returned to the wagon.

She picked up the empty pitcher and paused at the door.

"So when will you be taking the wood to her?"

"Tomorrow morning."

Lucy stopped the wagon behind the schoolhouse and the children clambered down, candy sacks in hand. She unhitched the horse to graze and slowly mounted the steps into what had been their home for the last nine months. Parting the curtain that hung across the front of the narrow room, she passed through from their meager quarters to the schoolroom proper. In spite of a good scrubbing, chalk dust lingered. The school board's need of a teacher had met her need of a livelihood, and they had been more than generous to let her live there. A form of charity, yet one she felt she had worked off. She straightened the inkwell and blotter on her desk, and resolve rippled up her spine on a sudden wash of memories.

Her mother had struggled alone after Pa left, taking in sewing and nearly blinding herself working long hours by lamplight. Lucy's good grades had spawned hopes of a better life. And when her classmate William Powell said he wanted to leave Chicago's swelter and go west, she accepted his proposal and went with him. One less mouth for her mother to feed. Now she faced near the same challenge.

In what remained of the day, Lucy started beans on the woodstove and loaded most of their belongings in the wagon. She set aside extra quilts for tomorrow's early departure. Cecilia and Elmore could sleep between the sacks and stores. Compared to the pallet on the floor they'd all shared, the wagon ride might be a luxury.

After a meal of biscuits and canned peaches, she put Cecilia and Elmore to bed early and sat outside on the small back stoop. Dusk dropped down with a sigh, and shadows tucked themselves beneath rocks and roots as she surveyed the small meadow. Crickets took up their chorus, doves joined with their melancholy song, and Mr. Wellington's words rolled over the grass. The Lord surely had taken care of her and the children through the long winter. And it had taken most of those months to loosen her grip on resentment.

God had not chosen to keep William alive—a fact with which Lucy was weary of wrestling. Death was not an uncommon visitor in this rugged land, but she'd not expected its sudden and brutal call at her home. Hugging her waist, she closed her eyes and let the evening breeze tug loosened hair and familiar words across her shoulders. *"Thou wilt shew me the path of life."* William had often repeated those words in their evening prayers, and for nine long months she had clung to them in his absence. Had he uttered them with his last breath—perhaps not for himself, but for her and the children? Was it his dying prayer she felt cooling her cheek?

Her job was to live, and to do so, she must accept that God knew what He was doing. She did not have to like it or agree with it. She just had to trust His love. If her children learned nothing else from her, they must learn that.

"Oh Lord, I am willing, but I need Your help." The breeze freshened, and she turned at the familiar caress. William had often touched her just as gently, and habit pulled her heart into her throat. She clenched her jaw. Too easily she could melt into a pool of self-pity. But such indulgence drained her strength and left her weak, and she dare not risk weakness if she and the children were to survive.

Chapter 3

Fumbling in the dark, Lucy buttoned an old house dress, tied on her bonnet, and pulled William's shotgun from beneath the pallet's edge. The change of clothing increased her excitement as she bundled her sleepy children into their makeshift bed. She stashed a fragrant pot of warm beans beneath the seat and took the road out of town.

Was she doing the right thing? Was it fair to Cecilia and Elmore to return to the mountain meadow William had so loved and try to make a go of it? Nearly every night she'd fallen asleep to the same question and wakened the next day with the same answer: *"Trust Me."* She hurled the whispered words into the darkness and listened as her doubts splintered beneath them.

The wagon stole past outlying houses and farms and

barking dogs, but her old mare paid no mind and plodded on, memory tugging her home. Dawn spilled over the hills as they climbed toward the higher ranges, and it warmed Lucy's back once they reached the little valley. A lacy green ribbon of bright aspen rimmed the meadow at the forest's edge, and knee-high grass skirted the barn and cabin, a silent invitation to snakes and other unwelcome guests. She shuddered.

Across the yard the barn door hung askew on a crooked hinge, loosened by winter storms. William's tools were in the tack room if no one had wandered through and taken them. She could fix the door. And chop the grass. And gather the cows. Her shoulders dipped. Oh Lord, how would she do it all? A light breeze fluttered around the wagon and ruffled the grass as she reined in near the cabin. Cecilia climbed over the bench seat, scrubbing her sleepy eyes. "We're home, Mama."

Home. Lucy kissed the top of her daughter's mussed hair then stilled at a dull thump coming from behind the cabin. Cecilia's eyes widened.

"What is it, Mama?"

"Shush." Lucy hurried her daughter back over the seat. "Cover your head and Elmore's, and don't make a sound," she whispered.

"But, Mama—"

"Hush. Do as I say."

Thump. . .thump.

With tingling arms she reached beneath the seat for the shotgun and climbed down. Gripping the gun in both hands, she cocked the hammer, pointed it ahead of her, and crept toward the building. She could shoot a bear if she had to, or a deer, but would a shotgun bring them down? That had to be what was making the noise—just an animal poking around. Her hands grew slick, and she wiped one on her skirt and then the other. No honey trees grew nearby, and it wasn't the time of year for bucks to be raking their antlers. She pushed her bonnet off, back pressed against the wall, and edged toward the corner. Sucking in a deep breath, she raised the gun to her shoulder. Lucy stepped into the open and drew a bead on. . .Buck Reiter.

The bearded bear of a man stood in his wagon and stared at her, firewood in each hand. "You're not gonna shoot me, are you?" He tossed the pieces on a pile between himself and the cabin, a dare burning in his eyes.

Lucy lowered the gun, fit to fly into him for ignoring her refusal and scaring her half to death. But he wasn't a real bear, or an outlaw, and for that she was grudgingly grateful. He bent for another log and tossed it on the pile. *Thump*.

"Mama, don't shoot!"

Lucy's trigger finger flinched at the high-pitched squeal, and she quickly aimed skyward. Whirling on her daughter, she bit back a fiery retort at the sight of the child's frightened expression. Elmore stood behind his sister, chewing on a suspender, his dark eyes shifting between Lucy and the man in the wagon.

Lucy let go her breath and dropped her arms. The gun's muzzle hit the ground and the world exploded.

Dirt flew up around them, and the children's screams tore the air as they rushed her. Clutching them close, Lucy fell to her knees. The wagon creaked, and pounding boots brought Buck Reiter to her side with a hand on her shoulder, warm and strong. She nearly melted beneath his touch.

Buck scanned the huddled bodies, looking for blood. "Are you all right?"

Two heads with dark saucer eyes answered with sober nods. Gently squeezing their mother's shoulder, he stuffed down the fear that had jerked him from the wagon. "And you, Mrs. Powell? Are you hurt?"

She shook her head and drew herself up. "I'm all right. J–just shaken."

He straightened and pulled his hat off to wipe the cold sweat from his forehead. Lord, have mercy, he thought she'd shot 'em all. The boy craned his neck back and squinted up at him, the first to recover. "Where'd you find all that wood, mister?"

Buck blew out a heavy breath and set his hat on. "Can you stack stove wood for your ma?" He pointed at the wall by the back porch. "Like I started there?"

The youngster shed his mother's clutches and ran for

the woodpile. "Sure can."

Mrs. Powell made to stand, and Buck helped with a hand to her elbow. Her face was white as a headstone, and her arm quivered beneath his fingers.

"Cecilia and I will unload our wagon." Sounding tougher than she looked, she brushed Buck with a wary glance and pulled her daughter closer.

He took a step back. "I can help if you need—"

"No." Sharp. Certain. "You've done more than enough already." Tugging at her bonnet ribbons, she pulled them from her neck.

He'd helped all right. Nearly got himself and the children shot. He picked up the gun, cracked it open, and kicked out the empty casing. "You have more shells?"

She stared at the weapon. "Yes... Yes, I have." Fumbling in her skirt, she withdrew another shell and handed it to him. "I'm sorry. I didn't expect to see you here and I heard the noise and I didn't know what to make of it and I..."

"No harm, ma'am." Her eyes simmered like black coffee. Strong and brave, in spite of the fright that shook her hands. He reloaded. "I'll set this inside the front door where it'll be handy in case you need it."

With a tight arm around her daughter's shoulder, she turned and walked around the end of the cabin as if she hadn't heard him.

Not exactly the way he'd hoped things would go.

Chapter 4

Still trembling, Lucy pulled the dutch oven from beneath the wagon seat and found the lid secure. How dare that man go against her expressed wishes that he not bring them firewood. He nearly got himself and her precious children buckshot. Shaking off the fear and anger, she wadded her skirt in her hands and grabbed the pot. "Open the door for me, and I'll set this on the table."

Cecilia pulled the latch, and the door squeaked open.

"Move over, honey. This is heavy." Lucy squeezed by and into the musty cabin, raising dust swirls with her boots. "Open the windows, and let's get some air in here, shall we?"

Setting the heavy cast iron on the table, she glanced back at her daughter who stood like a stone in the doorway. "Cecilia?"

The child blinked then ran to hide in Lucy's skirts. Lucy pulled her to the rocker and onto her lap, holding her as tightly as she held her own breath.

"I miss Papa." The thin voice pierced Lucy's heart, and she dipped her head against Cecilia's.

"I do, too." Closing her eyes, she searched for a comforting word to ease her daughter's sorrow and calm her own frayed nerves. Wood thumped against the cabin. "We are going to be just fine, sweetie. Help me get the things from the wagon. You can hang the quilts over the porch railing while I bring in our supplies."

Cecilia slid off her lap with a sniffle. "I want to be like you, Mama."

Lucy's throat tightened. "How?"

"I want to not cry."

"Oh, baby, I cry." She framed her daughter's face between her hands and thumbed the tear trails. "Crying is part of healing. It waters the dry places in our soul." She kissed the pert little nose. "Don't you be ashamed of your tears. Even Jesus cried."

"He did?"

Lucy nodded. "He knows what it feels like to miss someone we love."

Cecilia swiped at her cheeks and returned to the wagon, and Lucy tucked her words into her own heart. The Lord knew.

Soon they had the cabin dusted and swept, the rope

bed in the corner made up, and their extra things stored in the loft. Lucy sent Cecilia to the creek with a tin pitcher as Elmore scuttled inside with an armload of sticks. Mr. Reiter waited in the back doorway, hat in hand.

"Stack it neat. Don't want your ma tripping over anything while she's cooking."

Elmore piled the odd pieces and clapped dust from his hands.

"Good job, Button." The man's whiskers twitched.

Elmore frowned. "I ain't no button."

Her son's pout drew a chuckle from Mr. Reiter. Lucy went to the stove. "Elmore, you should say, 'I am not a button.'"

"I did." He locked his arms across his chest and scowled.

"That's what my pa called me when I was your age," Mr. Reiter said. "Button."

Elmore considered it then nodded once and turned to her. "Can we eat now?"

Oh, that all life's issues were solved so simply. She lifted the lid on the beans and stirred the contents, certain that Elmore's *we* included the stubborn man. Uninvited, but not unappreciated, he could eat in exchange for his labor. "The two of you need to wash up first, but I haven't primed the pump." She took a bucket from the corner and handed it to her son. "Rinse this out at the creek, then Mr. Reiter can help you fill it and bring it back. Cecilia's there now with a pitcher."

She looked the man's way and caught his smile as Elmore ran out the door. At least she thought he smiled. It was hard to tell with that buffalo robe he wore on his face.

She busied herself at the stove, feeding in the smallest pieces of wood and reaching to a high shelf where she felt for the matches. She hadn't thought about matches. What if there were none?

A footfall behind her, and Mr. Reiter's long arm produced the match box. This time she saw a smile for certain, with him standing so close she could smell the sunshine and sweat from his shirt. "Thank you." More words came before he stepped outside. "You are welcome to eat with us."

He paused with a hand on the door frame and looked over his shoulder. "Thank you kindly."

Relief trilled through her at his acceptance, surprising her as it doused her earlier resentment. Uninvited or not, Mr. Reiter's presence delayed the inevitable. Her fatherless family would soon be alone, far from town tonight and for many more nights to come.

Baked beans and biscuits greeted Buck on his return with the children. Cecilia managed to get a half-filled pitcher back and a pocketful of wild strawberries. Elmore's mouth was red with what she couldn't reach first, and Buck helped the boy haul the bucket inside and set it in the sink.

Four plates topped the plank table, with spoons and cups at each. A bowl of canned peaches sat in the center with a plate of golden biscuits and a pot of beans. Feeling as handy as a leash on a polecat, Buck held his hat against his stomach and waited by the hearth on the opposite side of the room.

Mrs. Powell poured creek water in the tin cups then took her seat. The children settled in with ease, leaving empty the chair at the end. Three pairs of eyes looked his way.

"Ma makes the best beans. Don't you want none?"

"Don't you want *any*, Elmore."

"Yes, Ma, I sure do."

Cecilia giggled, and her ma appeared to choke back a laugh. Welcoming the lighter mood, Buck took the remaining chair. Cecilia slipped from her seat, delicately lifted his hat, and hung it on a row of hooks by the front door. "Pa always hung his hat there," she said on her return. "I s'pose you can do the same."

Grateful for the beard that hid his discomfort, Buck cleared his throat. "Thank you."

The children bowed their heads, and he did the same.

"For this food we give Thee thanks. Amen." Three voices recited the brief prayer, one with a tight edge. Buck raised his head and kept his eyes on the peaches, away from the determined woman to his left.

After dinner Lucy and the children cleared the table. Buck primed the pump with a ladleful of water from the bucket, and soon well water pulled up clear and sweet.

"Thank you, Mr. Reiter." Lucy stood by the table, her hands resting on a chair back. The set of her jaw and shoulders had eased a bit, and she looked downright weary.

"My pleasure, ma'am, but I'd like to ask you a favor."

Her schoolmarm brows snapped together then smoothed as she caught herself. "You may."

He took his hat from the peg. "Please, call me Buck, ma'am. Mr. Reiter was my pa, and I feel old when you and the children call me that."

Elmore stepped close and cocked his head back for a better look. "But you got an old beard."

"Elmore!" Lucy's face flushed, and she drew the boy to her. "That is not polite."

Buck grinned and stroked the bushy mass. " 'Out of the mouths of babes,' they say." Babes and his sister. He chucked the boy's chin and headed outside to finish stacking wood.

Pausing on the porch, he drank in the forested sweep that rose above them to the west. Sweet pinion and juniper perfumed the air, and he pulled in a deep draught. Behind him water gushed into the sink, Cecilia giggled, and chairs scraped their way under the table. Sounds of home. A home that wasn't his. An empty spot in his chest tore a little wider, and he rubbed the ache. Time to be heading out.

Elmore bounded through the door and bowled into him. "Come on, Mr. Buck. I wanna show you the barn." Small fingers clasped his hand and pulled him toward the neglected structure. He hefted the boy up and onto his shoulders.

Inside, a flattened pile of musty hay littered one dark corner. Stall doors gaped, and dried-out tack hung from one wall. A small room held a workbench and tools that waited for their owner to put them to task. "Duck your head," he said as he tucked down to step through the door.

"Them's Pa's tools." Two chubby arms clamped around Buck's neck as he smoothed the long handle of a hammer. "Ma says he's gone and not coming back. Said he died in the woods."

Buck lifted the boy off his shoulders and set him on the ground then squatted before him, eye to eye in the slatted light. "It's hard not getting to see the people you love." He straightened a sagging suspender over one small shoulder. "I know someone else who lost his pa, too, but he grew up to be a fine, strong man. So will you."

Elmore stared at the dirt floor and shoved his hands in his pockets.

Buck stood and reached for the hammer. "If you remember where your pa kept the nails, we can fix the big door."

Elmore cocked his head and looked up at him. "Pa was good at fixin' things, too." Then he stepped up on an overturned box and reached for a tin at the back of the workbench. "He used these long ones for the doors."

Buck gathered a handful and dropped them in his vest pocket. "Bring that box you're standing on and you can help drive the nails."

Shadows licked across the yard as Buck and Elmore patched the barn, and cooler air pulled through the open doors on each end. Soon the evening breeze signaled a ride over the near ridge and back to Horne Ranch. As Buck returned the tools and took a final look around, a slender silhouette marked the entry.

"Would you like to stay to supper?"

Weariness rippled through her voice like a dying stream, and one hand rubbed her shoulder at the base of her neck. He'd like to stay forever.

"I expect they'll be watching for me at the ranch." He'd not take more of her food. "But thank you just the same."

She closed the door after him, and with Elmore in hand, followed as Buck climbed in the wagon and gathered the reins. The boy broke away and ran to the wheel.

"You comin' back tomorrow?"

Buck's insides knotted, and he glanced at the young widow. Her jaw held firm as did her stance, but no resistance filled her eyes.

"If it's all right with your ma."

Elmore whirled around. "It's all right with you, ain't it, Ma?"

A near smile broke, and she nodded. Cecilia joined her and stood close, their skirts touching.

Buck slapped Rose ahead and tugged his hat brim. Lucy Powell stood with a hand pressing each child against her, watching him as if he'd tied up the daylight itself and was dragging it out of her world.

Chapter 5

Lucy lay awake between her children, their shallow breath rising together as one. She rubbed calloused hands over her face, her muscles aching from the unaccustomed work. But these moments of predawn peace were priceless, for in them she heard the Lord's soft whisper again: "*Trust me.*"

The storms made it difficult.

Every afternoon for a week they had rolled in over the mountains, each thunder clap and lightning strike reminding her of what she'd lost and how. She could bear the hard work, her dried and cracked hands, even the pain in her neck. But the storms mocked her, delivering again the blow of losing William.

Slipping from the bed, she checked each angelic

face before padding to the stove and stoking the fire for coffee. Water flowed freely into the pot, and Buck came to mind, his bulk filling the kitchen corner as he primed the pump. As he sat at the table's head. As he chucked Elmore under the chin and tugged Cecilia's braids. If a body were to judge by outward appearances, one would think Buck Reiter liked being around her family. If a body were to judge by hidden feelings, one would think Lucy liked having him around. Somehow his presence lessened the drudgery.

Thin light seeped above the eastern ridge, and she quickly dressed and pulled on her boots. As she tied off the end of her braid, a wagon rolled into the yard and stopped at the barn. Elmore would be thrilled.

After returning the second and third day as Elmore had requested, Buck had since been gone for four. Each morning the child hung from the porch railing, dangling his feet off the edge, waiting for the familiar wagon to drive up the road. And each morning it did not come he'd gone about his chores like a lost pup. Yes, Elmore would be happy. So would Cecilia.

Lucy's insides fluttered as she ground the coffee and added it to the pot. Glancing at her sleeping children, she slipped out the back door, surprised that she hadn't yet adjusted to the altitude. She couldn't quite get her wind.

The horse stood tied to the hitching rail at the barn,

and Buck pulled long planks from the wagon and stacked them against the outer wall. Even in the new light, Lucy could make out posts and crates and covered baskets in the bed. Grumbling hens clucked their displeasure at being caged, and she bristled. *Charity.*

She marched to the wagon, ready to tell him to take everything back. But he turned at her approach and his eyes brightened like the dawning sky. Pride melted into a pool of warm butter.

"Mornin'." His beard puffed out on each side in what she'd learned was a smile.

"Good morning." She gripped the edges of her apron. "This really is too much." His eyes disarmed her, bore right through her, until a scratching whimper drew her aside. From a crate at the end of the wagon, a pink tongue licked between the slats. Buck lowered the board and pulled the crate to the edge. "I figured your young'uns needed a young'un of their own." He gave her a sidelong look. "Hope you don't mind. We don't need two dogs at our place."

Mind? How could she mind? In fact, where *was* her mind? Holding her fingers against the slats, she sniffed a laugh at the quick washing. "Seems a happy fellow." Next to her, Buck released a tight breath. Did he really seek her approval?

He opened the crate and a black-and-white puppy wriggled over the top and into Lucy's arms before she could refuse it. Climbing her body, it stretched to lick her chin and draw her laughter. "What a rascal you are!"

Buck retrieved the squirming bundle and set it on the ground. "That's as good a name as any. Rascal." He skewered the pup with a blue glare. "You mind your manners."

The puppy skittered around the wagon, sniffing and pawing. What a delight for the children! Lucy brushed her bodice and apron and caught Buck appraising her reaction. Preparing to voice her concerns, she straightened her shoulders.

"I can never repay you for your kindness—for all you've done for us."

"I'm not lookin' for repayment, ma'am. Just lookin' to help a neighbor."

Dare she believe him? "Why?" The hard word felt heavy on her tongue, but she needed to know before he did more. Before she imagined the wrong motivation. Few men did anything without thought of recompense.

He pulled his hat off and ran a hand over his wheat-colored hair. "Good Book says to help widows and orphans"—he looked her straight in the eye—"and the way I see it, you qualify."

His words pressed a bitter barb in her wounded heart. What had she expected? Affection? Enjoyment of her company? She drew a deep breath and raised her chin. At least he wouldn't be forcing himself on her. She made to turn away, and he stopped her with a light touch on her arm.

"I like helping you, ma'am. You and those babies of yours. I enjoy doing what I can for you. But if I make you uncomfortable, just tell me and I'll move on."

His eyes clouded, and a crease formed between his brows. At such a contrast from his greeting, she felt near guilty for stealing what joy she'd seen earlier. A sudden decision fell from her lips before she could reconsider. "Call me Lucy. 'Ma'am' is so formal."

His whiskers bulged, and his brow smoothed. "Lucy, then." He shoved his hat on and looked at the pup scratching around his feet. "Rascal here shouldn't be too much extra work for you. He'll do on table scraps and help keep the critters from your cabin."

The man thought of everything, like a good friend. Her shoulders relaxed. "Let me help you." He could handle three times or more the weight she could carry, but still she reached for a pole. Together they dragged it out and started a second pile next to the barn. "What are your plans for all of this?"

"The chicken coop needs repair—looks likes coyotes dug in." He turned to face the garden she'd worked to resurrect. "Deer fence needs work." He grazed her with a quick glance. "I brought a bag of seed spuds." He paused and looked away. "And I see you've got some pie plants coming on—"

His gaze jerked to the wagon. "I almost forgot." Two long strides took him to the front where he lifted a handled basket and presented it like a gift. "Lemons. Lilly said she had plenty."

Lucy took the basket and peeked beneath the checkered cloth, stalling to stuff her emotions back in place. Lemonade. How appropriate. Her mouth watered with the bitterness of endless work and the sweetness of this man's kindness. Pulling a rare smile from her heart, she looked into his sky-filled eyes.

"Do you like hotcakes?"

Chapter 6

Hotcakes. Cold cakes. Any kind of cake Lucy Powell offered, he'd take. Just thinking her name left Buck feeling as spur-tangled as his nephew last fall after bringing Ara home in a snowstorm. Buck just never thought the same thing would happen to an old bronc like him.

He pulled his fingers through his beard. Wasn't white, but it *looked* old, according to Button. It hadn't mattered till Buck ran into the boy's mother at the mercantile. She had to be ten years younger than him, but if she worked this place by herself, she wouldn't look it for long. Wasn't right for a woman to use herself up on hard work—man's work. And if he had any say in it, she wouldn't.

Elmore nearly bowled him over in the yard, and Buck

snagged him and dangled him upside down. Didn't know a boy could laugh so hard or hug so tight. And when he and his sister saw Rascal, Buck thought they'd squeal themselves silly. Made his throat tight, and he walked into the barn for a spell to check the hinges on the stall doors.

Not long after, a sweet ribbon of fried bacon drew him to the cabin, and it was hard to say which was better—the hot coffee Lucy poured or the warm smile that accompanied it. Her braid hung over her shoulder, and he wanted to run it through his fingers like a horse's mane. She might not think kindly of the comparison, but that was the closest he'd come to long fine hair such as hers.

By midmorning he and Elmore had the chicken yard repaired, and he carried a slatted crate inside the small henhouse. "She's setting," he told the boy, "so you best not be reaching under her for eggs."

Elmore peered beneath the nest. "When will they hatch?"

Buck eased the crate into a corner. "Maybe not at all if she leaves off setting after being moved like this. But you keep an eye on her, and let me know how things go."

He brought the other cage from the wagon, set it on the ground, and released a trio of pullets and a young rooster. "If she doesn't hatch that clutch, she'll get another chance with this fella here."

Elmore eyed the small comb and red wattle. "Ma says roosters don't lay eggs."

Buck backed away from that prickly pear and hurried

to the wagon with the empty cage. He'd not be getting into such things with Elmore. His ma was a teacher. She could educate him on the ways of hens and roosters.

Flushed at his close escape and talk of nature's ways, he reset his hat and pulled on his thick work gloves. Elmore joined him as he grabbed a roll of barbed wire. "Can you step off your ma's garden and show me the boundaries?"

The boy's whole face grinned, and he picked up the napping puppy and ran off around the cabin.

Lucy brought a water crock and ladle to the back porch, tied on her bonnet, and with Cecilia set to work weeding the garden. Later, when she straightened to rub her neck and shoulder, Buck's pulse hitched at the sight, and he made for the porch and the dipper. A new thirst was burning its way through his chest, but it had nothing to do with water and everything to do with brave, beautiful Lucy Powell. His plans to leave began to lose their luster, and he could hardly imagine the rumble of horses' hooves across distant pastures any longer.

After dinner, Elmore held posts while Buck tamped them in, and by supper time they had the garden fenced and a few hills of potatoes. While Lucy watched from the porch, he showed Cecilia and Elmore how to plant them. "Might take three weeks for the fuzzy leaves to appear, but don't be digging them up to peek."

Cecilia giggled, and Elmore threw her an irritated look. Reminded Buck of him and Lilly when they were sprouts. He stood and brushed the dirt from his knees. The children ran off to play with Rascal, and Buck dropped a wire loop from the gate around the end post. More-determined critters would make it through, but at least the deer wouldn't ravage all their work.

Lucy waited on the porch, and he could feel her eyes runnin' over him like cool water on a hot day. Lord, help him. What had he expected when he set out to help a widow and her young'uns? It for sure wasn't what churned through him every time he thought of her.

"Stay for supper?"

Her quiet invitation nearly pulled his heart up through his gullet, and he approached slowly, deliberately, until he met her eye to eye where she stood on the porch. He longed to touch her, but instead drank in every feature of her face, hoping to slake his thirst.

"I best be getting back before dark to help Nate with chores." Nate didn't need help, but Buck needed to leave. Needed to keep things right between him and Lucy Powell, even if it drove him loco. She tipped her head and smiled that sweet-water way she had that closed up his throat and made him sweat. It'd be so easy to lean in and taste her lips.

"Thank you for all your help." She touched his arm. "Be careful going home."

Home. He could find it right here if she'd have him. He swallowed hard. "Just got one ridge to cross." And one porch rail and one decade. He swallowed again. "Tell Button and Sissy to make sure Rascal has plenty of water." Like she wouldn't know that herself. But what else was he going to say—*I love you, Lucy Powell?*

He stepped back with a brief nod and worked at not running for the wagon. But he rode hard through all the advice he'd given Nate last fall. *"Tell Ara how you feel,"* he'd said, all bold and brassy when it wasn't his own heart at the snubbin' post.

By the time Buck pulled onto the Horne Ranch road, coyote chatter had chased daylight over the hills. His sweaty shirt had cooled, and he pulled at his beard and scratched his cheek. Nate was waiting for him in the front porch rocker, feet up on the rail and wearing a grin to rival Elmore's.

Buck knew what was coming. He just didn't know what to say to it.

Chapter 7

Lucy scorched the coffee, burned the hotcakes, and nearly wore a hole in her apron rubbing her hands on it. Her heart beat like a running rabbit when she closed her eyes and saw him again—standing so close she could smell his scent and the toil he'd spent on her and the children. She longed to hold her hand against his face, beard and all, and kiss his sweaty brow. Oh Lord, how could she have such feelings?

"Mama, are you all right?"

Lucy's eyes flew open with a guilty start. She owed her children more than to swoon at the table over a man she had no business even thinking about. "Yes, Sissy, just resting my eyes." Her mother's weary words so often repeated spilled from her lips without thought. Resting her heart was more like it. Resting it in daydreams of a kind man's tenderness and help. She picked up her coffee, tepid and bitter. *Oh, Buck. Why did you leave us alone?*

She yanked back the unspoken words. No—not Buck, William. Her hand trembled as she set down her cup.

Cecilia poked her blackened cakes, and Elmore picked up his and tore off a chunk. Neither complained, but Lucy knew what dampened their childish hearts. Buck had not been back for a week. She pushed her plate aside and added another spoon of sugar to the thick coffee. At least the chickens would eat the burned cakes. Chickens Buck had brought, thriving in a henhouse Buck had repaired. Everywhere she looked and everything she did brought him to mind. His bushy face had pushed William's countenance from her memory, and guilt weighed as heavy as her responsibilities. But William wasn't there to laugh and play with the children and work beside her and hold her in a blue gaze until she thought she would melt with longing.

Now, neither was Buck.

She missed him desperately. Not just his helpful labor, but him. The way his eyes twinkled when he teased the children. The way they warmed when he looked at her. The touch of his rough hand on her shoulder and the heat it sent clear through to her bones.

Rascal rumbled into her thoughts with a fierce puppy growl. The children looked at each other and then at Lucy. She scooted back and went for the shotgun. Cracking the door, she scanned the yard between the cabin and barn then saw the lone rider coming across the pasture. Rascal joined her, ears cocked as he sniffed at the door. His sharp yap made her flinch, and she signaled Cecilia, who scurried to the door and took the pup to the loft.

"Lord, protect us," she whispered as Elmore followed his sister up the ladder.

The stranger neared the cabin, and Lucy gripped the gun with both hands. Still blistered from the incident on their first day, she held it steady as she eased her foot in front of the door, aiming just shy of the rider. He didn't slow his pace but steadily walked his horse until it reached the hitching rail and stopped as if it belonged there.

The broad shoulders. The hat shading his eyes.

"It's Mr. Buck! It's Mr. Buck!"

Lucy jerked at the sharp squeal from above but managed to lower the muzzle without blowing a hole in the man. Twice she'd had him at the wrong end of a shotgun. The children clambered down the ladder and stormed past her, jumping up and down on the wood-plank porch.

"You're back. You're back," Elmore chanted. "I knew you'd come back."

A grin split the man's face in two, and his blue eyes locked on to Lucy, drawing the very breath from her lungs.

"You cut off your beard," Cecilia said. "Can I feel?"

"Sissy!" Mortified, Lucy stepped outside.

Buck swung from the saddle and took a knee on the

bottom step. "You sure can."

The children launched into his arms, and he tossed his head back with a warm laugh. Lucy shivered. Elmore pressed his hand against the smooth face, and Buck's eyes closed, his firm mouth lifting in delight.

Lucy leaned the gun against the house and hid her own hands in her skirts to keep from doing what her heart wanted. If she touched that dear face, she would likely kiss it, and then what would her children think?

"Do you like it?" Buck's question refocused her.

Cecilia tilted her head. "You got younger."

Elmore stepped back and thumbed his suspenders like a little man. "It's fine by me."

Buck stood and removed his hat, mauling it in his rough grip. "And you, Lucy?" His deep voice resonated through her. "Is it fine by you?"

Her thudding heart drew her fingers to her throat. "Yes. . .but I didn't know you. I mean. . ."

"I'd hoped you'd like it." His mouth tipped. "At least enough not to shoot me off my horse."

His teasing loosened her nerves and drained away her anxiety. Elmore grasped Buck's fingers and tugged him down, cupping a hand against his mouth with a loud whisper. "Did you cut off your beard so Ma would kiss ya?"

Buck choked at Lucy's horrified look, but he refused

to laugh at her expense. For once, she had no teacherly words to come to her aid. He stepped up on the porch and chucked the boy's chin. Both children giggled, and Lucy flushed. Pretty as a filly in a flower bed, she was, standing there with rosy cheeks and her apron knotted in her hands. She looked everywhere but at him.

"I, uh. . .would you like some coffee?" she asked his horse.

"Don't know about Charlie, but I'd be obliged."

Her head jerked around. "Charlie?"

"My horse."

"Ma, you know horses don't drink coffee." Elmore grabbed her hand and pulled.

"Oh, shush, you." She tousled his hair and pushed him ahead of her into the cabin.

Sissy lingered. "Whatcha got in your poke?"

The girl didn't miss a lick. "Flowers for your ma." He untied the saddle strings holding the bag.

"That's a funny way to carry flowers."

Dropping to one knee, he opened the bag and carefully folded the edges down around the rich dark soil and a cluster of blue-and-white flowers. "They're columbines. Do you think she'll like them?"

"Oh, yes, Mr. Buck. I *know* she will."

"Where should we plant them?"

Brightening at his *we*, she smoothed her skirt like her mother. "I know just the place." She dashed off the end of the porch and around the corner, and he found her by a sheltered spot near the back door.

"Good choice."

"I'll get the shovel." She sprinted for the barn.

When the task was completed, Sissy stood back with her hands on her waist like a little Lucy. Then she rushed through the back door.

"Mama, come see what Mr. Buck brought you."

Through the open doorway, Buck saw Lucy dry her hands on her apron and push at her hair. She followed Sissy outside to the end of the porch, and again a hand fussed at her throat and her cheeks pinked the moment she saw the flowers.

"They're lovely, Buck."

Hope sparked at the softness of her voice.

"I helped plant them." Sissy beamed. Lucy hugged the girl and cut a glance his way that fanned the spark. Spotting that bunch of blue at the edge of the meadow was sure enough worth having to dig it up with his knife.

"Coffee's almost ready. And I have biscuits, too, if you're hungry."

Hunger didn't begin to describe what swirled through his middle. "Thank you kindly."

Elmore scooted by with a can of scraps, and Buck stepped inside and took a seat in the rocking chair. The smell of charred coffee gave way to fresh beans that Lucy ground. His hands itched for a willow branch, and he looked around the cabin as if he'd find a peeled piece just waiting to be whittled. A curtain draped back from a bed, and a braided rug covered the floor beside it. Fancy plates leaned against a hutch back, and a large trunk sat beneath the front window with a shelf full of books close by.

Lucy didn't chatter as she worked, and he watched her the same way he watched cottontails scatter at sunup or deer drinking at a stream. A small hand touched his arm. Sissy stood close with a yellow-haired doll. "Pa used to set me on his knee and rock my baby to sleep."

A tight gasp flitted across the small room, and Lucy turned with startled eyes. Buck lifted the child to his lap. "Like this?" He pushed against the floor and the chair tipped slowly back and forth. She leaned against his chest and stroked her doll's golden curls, so unlike her own dark braids. Then she sighed and nodded her head in silent assent. He curled his arm around her and his gaze met Lucy's. Did she resent him? Was he stepping into her husband's place, disregarding his memory? He held her eyes and saw a yearning there that burned clean through him. He had half a mind to hope it might have something to do with him.

While Lucy set plates, butter, and biscuits on the table and poured the coffee, Cecilia fell into a deep sleep. Lucy came softly, bending down, her eyes grazing his lips as she slipped her arms beneath the child. Then she regarded him steadily and mouthed the words, *Thank you.*

Fighting for a solid breath, Buck made his way to the table and took a seat. Elmore climbed into the closest chair, and Rascal curled in a ball beneath him.

"Rascal let us know you was here."

"*Were* here," Lucy whispered as she passed behind her son and on to her chair. This time she held her hands out, one across the table for Elmore and one for Buck. Accustomed to the practice at his sister's table, he grasped Button's tiny hand in his, and with the other, Lucy's slender fingers. Her touch sent his thoughts as far from table grace as snow is from summer.

"For this food we give Thee thanks," she said quietly. "And thank You for bringing Buck safely to us this morning. Amen."

He waited, head bowed, not willing to let go. Lucy withdrew her hand and reached for the platter. She dropped a golden round onto her son's plate and turned to Buck. "Two or three?"

Chapter 8

Lucy's fluttering emotions spread to her serving hand, and she prayed Buck didn't notice. What would she tell him? That the columbines matched his eyes? That he made her achingly mindful of a strong and thoughtful man in her home again? Heat crept up her neck, and she left the table on pretense of warming the already hot coffee.

Upon her return, she found Buck had eaten the three biscuits she'd given him and was reaching for another.

"Lilly invited you and the children to the ranch next Saturday. With Ara in the family way, we're not driving into town for the Fourth of July festivities, so Lilly's making pies and chocolate cake for our own celebration."

"Whatcha mean 'family way'?" Elmore asked.

Buck choked on his biscuit.

"Elmore." Lucy stifled her laughter at Buck's discomfort. "Shush, and eat your breakfast."

"But Ma—"

"Now." She eyed her son into submission, dabbed her mouth with a napkin, and turned to Buck. "What can I bring?"

A bit ruddier without his beard, he busied himself with his coffee then cleared his throat. "Yourself and the children."

Pinning him with a long look, she folded her arms. Truth was, she appreciated the opportunity to stare. "We will not go unless we can contribute to the celebration." Perplexity made him even more attractive. He didn't take his eyes from hers, but they searched deep, as if trying to find a breach in a rocked-up canyon. Finally, he huffed in resignation.

"Baked beans."

The duel ended when she laughed, and his handsome face pulled a worried frown. "Something wrong with baked beans?"

She laughed again and reached for his hand resting on the table, as if such a move were as natural as taking a breath. "Baked beans it is."

He caught her fingers, and his warmth and strength seeped into all her cold and empty places. "I'll come for you early, and you can spend the day."

Scrabbling for self-sufficiency, she withdrew her hand. "We have a wagon, you know. Just tell us how to find your place."

His mouth opened then clamped shut, and his jaw tightened. Lucy balled her apron in her lap but held her head steady. Buck glanced at Elmore, the biscuits, and then settled his blue gaze on her with another huff. "Take your road to the ridge, then turn north and follow the trail about three miles. I'll wait for you at the top."

A compromise, but it suited her. She exhaled and smiled. "We'll leave at sunup."

By early afternoon, Lucy had sent the children to the creek to hunt strawberries. She still had the lemons, and wild-berry lemonade would be perfect for the Fourth of July if the berries lasted another week. Buck worked on the steps leading into the root cellar, and Lucy joined him with a bucket of water, lye soap, and a rag to give the shelves a good cleaning. A distant rumble froze her feet. She turned to scan the range sweeping north of the wide valley, where steel-gray clouds bellied over the ridge. A sudden wind whipped across the meadow and tugged at her hair and skirts. Buck set his hat and cut her a look. She dropped the bucket and ran for the creek.

Buck closed the cellar door and took Lucy's bucket and soap to the back porch. He then secured the barn and henhouse. Her sudden dash hinted at more than caution, and he ached to see a common squall upset her so. But it hadn't quite been a year, according to Lilly, since lightning had taken her husband.

By the time he returned from the barn, the children were on the porch and Lucy had planted herself in the middle of the garden. Her hands balled into fists, and she lifted her head to the storm as if she could hold it off by sheer will—one woman against all of nature's thunderous power. If he'd learned anything about Lucy Powell in four short weeks, that was exactly her intention.

The fast-moving storm rolled down the wooded slopes and dropped into the valley. Lightning fired a warning shot, but Lucy stood fast. Buck gripped the porch railing and glanced at Sissy and Button standing stock-still near the doorway. He loved this family more than he thought possible—Lucy with her fight and fire, and those two young'uns who worshipped the light she walked in. He had hoped to cut their hay this summer, but from the looks of the white wall coming at them, he might not get the chance.

The clouds unfolded, banked against the opposite mountains and packed down like a feather mattress. Rain came gentle at first, errant drops, plump and singular. Lucy stood like a ship's mast, wind whipping her skirt through her legs. Buck screwed his hat down and strode to the gate but waited, holding himself back from her private war. Gorged to its limit, the sky broke open, and within minutes water ran like a river. The meager garden floated in a dark lake that licked at Lucy's skirts. When the hail came, her hands went slack and her shoulders slumped. She dropped to her knees.

Lucy Powell didn't want to be coddled, but he'd not stand by and watch her drown in defeat. Splashing into the running current, he scooped her into his arms and offered his back to the stinging fury. Ice the size of checker pieces pelted into every living plant, beating them into the muddy water.

Wide-eyed and white as sheets, Sissy and Button followed him inside where he fell into the rocker with their mother. Her great wracking sobs gouged his heart like Mexican spurs, and he jerked off his dripping hat and leaned back, pulling her closer. She pressed into him, trembling, he suspected, with more than the cold and wet. Her hair was smooth against his lips, and he murmured low, aiming to calm her as he would a frightened colt.

The children stood mute by the table, staring at their strong, independent mother curled up in Buck's arms. Thunder cracked, and the windows flashed a blinding blue. They ran and flung themselves against him, and he drew them close like a covey of rain-soaked quail. Huddled together in the sturdy cabin, they waited, and Buck thanked God for seeing fit to lead him there.

As quick as it had come, the storm tucked tail and ran.

Lucy had soaked him through, but she no longer shivered or sobbed. Outside, blue sky peeked through running clouds and sunlight winked in the water dripping from the roof.

"Button," he whispered, "can you build a fire for your ma?"

The boy peeled himself from the rocker and shoved out his thin chest with a nod. "Yes, sir, I can."

Buck returned the nod, man-to-man. "Then be about it."

Sissy laid a small hand on her mother's back. "You need to get out of those wet clothes, Mama." The girl's brow pulled with motherly concern. "I'll help you."

Lucy uncurled but didn't fly from his lap. Instead, she cupped her daughter's cheek in her hand. "Thank you, honey. Lay out my black dress, and I'll be right there."

Then she turned her eyes on Buck, and the aching, brimming pools stopped his heart.

"I can't do this anymore," she whispered.

He caught her hand in his and turned it over. Blistered, red, and cracking, the palm bore testimony to her determined spirit. He raised it to his lips fearing only one thing—seeing her break.

"Not by yourself, you can't." His voice felt thick and unfamiliar. "But *we* can."

A heavy sigh shuddered through her. "You are a kind man, Buck Reiter."

He locked on her eyes, refusing to let her slip into despair. "Two are better than one, the Lord says." A current surged between them, swift as the water through the garden. Did she feel it?

Standing, he set her feet to the floor then curled his fingers against her cheek. She tilted her head into his touch, and he would have kissed her had Cecilia not returned to lead her to the curtained-off bedroom. As daughter and mother crossed the room, Buck's jaw set like a sulled-up bronc. He'd stay and see them through the summer, find their cows and brand the calves. Salvage what he could of the hay and the garden, and wait for Lucy Powell's heart to heal.

Then he'd ask her to be his wife.

Chapter 9

The pale pink muslin hid near the bottom of Lucy's trunk, beneath baby clothes and linens she had saved against a better day. She'd not worn the dress since last summer, before she'd donned her mourning black. Pressing the cool fabric to her face, she squeezed her eyes shut to hold the tears.

Last week's hail had shredded not only the garden but had torn deeply into her resolve. Already July, and what little progress she'd made lay pounded into the mud. At least the outbuildings stood undamaged, thanks to Buck, upon whom she could not depend indefinitely. Someday he would not return. She had no right to wish otherwise.

She draped the muslin across her arm and pulled out

Cecilia's church dress and Elmore's good trousers then gathered a handful of pins and headed outside to air the garments.

A pungent sweetness swept down from the mountains, kissing the meadow. Her skin prickled in the cool air as she took in her surroundings with new eyes. How many horses could graze here and in her higher acreage? Buck had once mentioned his intent to take his band of mares and find his own mountain, as he'd put it. Would he be interested in leasing her land? And if he did, where would she and the children go? But why would he want to settle so near the Horne Ranch when he said he wanted new country? Her heart hollowed out at the thought of his leaving.

If she could sell off some of her cattle in the fall, she might make a go of it this year. But she had to find them first. Buck had set out early to locate the small herd, and suggested she ride with him after the Fourth to bring them back. The children could stay with his sister who, he insisted, would jump at the opportunity. What a temptation—a day riding the hills with no cares other than trailing a few cows. She'd promised to give it some thought, and when she'd mentioned it to Cecilia and Elmore, they had stormed her with pleas.

Before the hail, she had looked forward to the Fourth of July, celebrating not only the nation's independence but her own. She wanted to visit with Buck's sister and learn her secret of surviving as a widowed mother in this harsh land. But Lucy already knew the answer.

A heavy sigh slid over Cecilia's dress as Lucy pinned it to the garden wire Buck had raised. He'd raised the woodpile, too, and she'd allowed him to raise her hopes of success and more. But she wasn't his sister. She wasn't his anything. His "two are better than one" remark referred to how they had worked—side by side as two individuals. Not two parts of one whole.

The only thing Lucy knew with certainty was the way she'd felt in Buck's arms after the storm. Safe. Protected. A bitter taste hit the back of her tongue.

"Oh, Mama—do I get to wear my Sunday dress to Mr. Buck's house?" Cecilia's hopeful voice pinched Lucy's heart.

"You must promise not to ruin it. No grass stains or rips, please."

Cecilia clasped her hands beneath her chin. "I promise."

Lucy turned to scan the sky then placed a hand on her daughter's shoulder. "Remember those strawberries?"

Delight sparked in the child's eyes, and she nodded.

"Take Elmore with you and pick what you can. But pay attention to what you hear. If it thunders, come home immediately. Understand?"

Cecilia nodded fiercely then hugged Lucy's legs and dashed to the house for a basket and her brother. Lucy's gaze fell to the columbine cluster at the end of the porch, so fragile and lovely, untouched by the hail in its sheltered corner.

"The path of life, Lord," she whispered. "I need to know the path of life."

Again the words came, whispering across the meadow and dancing around her shoulders. *"Trust me."*

The aroma of sweet beans drew Lucy from bed before dawn. She set the iron pot on the sideboard, punched down the bread dough she'd left to rise, and pinched off rounds to bake while she hitched up the horse. The children stirred and excitement rimmed their faces as they hurried to dress in their sun-kissed clothes. Even her pink muslin smelled fresh and clean from its airing out. Hope stirred. With shaking fingers she twisted her hair, dropping more pins than usual. Elmore picked up each one, and with the last coil in place, she chucked his chin.

"Thank you, Button." *Buck's gesture. Buck's nickname.* "You are a big help."

"I never seen you drop so many pins before, Ma."

Her heart would break for love. "Saw. You never *saw*." She leaned down to kiss his sweet head and swatted him toward the sink. "Take the scrap can to the chickens, but don't get dirty, and hurry back. We want to leave before the sun peeks over the ridge."

Cecilia took the rolls from the oven, carefully shielding

her small hands with toweling, and set them on the sideboard. "You sure look pretty, Ma." She lined a basket with a napkin and arranged the rolls just so. "Did you dress up for Mr. Buck?"

Lucy's breath caught. "I dressed up for the occasion. Just like you." Reaching for another piece of toweling, she lifted the cast-iron pot.

"But you do like Mr. Buck, don't you?"

What had he said? Out of the mouths of babes? Her throat ached. "Yes, I like Mr. Buck."

"Is he going to be our pa?"

The dutch oven landed on the table with a thud. Now was not the time to discuss such things, but a six-year-old did not have a keenly developed sense of timing. Lucy swallowed a scolding and instead chose truth. Stooping to meet her daughter face-to-face, she looked into William's eyes, and sorrow tightened like a drawstring.

"A lady waits until a man asks to marry her. You will do that someday—wait for a young man to ask for your hand." Taking that small hand, she smoothed it with her own. "Mr. Buck is very special to us all." Warmth bloomed in Lucy's chest, pressing to expose more than she cared to admit. "I believe God sent him to help us, but whether he wants to be part of our family is up to him. And neither you nor I will ask him about it."

Cecilia blinked. "But would you say yes if Mr. Buck asked?"

Lucy closed her eyes, attempting to close off her heart from her daughter's keen perception. Squeezing the small hand, she opened them again with purpose. "Do you want to be late for the party?"

Instantly refocused, Cecilia gathered her basket and hurried to the wagon. Lucy followed with the beans then returned to the cabin for her wild-berry lemonade. Two contrasting halves made one delicious whole—berries and lemons. And Buck had provided one of those halves. Was there anything in her life he had not touched?

As they drove from the yard, a sharp golden light cut across the mountains, and Lucy tugged her bonnet forward. Elmore held Rascal on his lap and Cecilia cradled the basket. Not one word of complaint came from either of them, not with Independence Day breaking clear and bright with the promise of pie and cake and maybe games. Lucy shook her head. How little they knew of true independence—of leaning only on one's self and not another for everything. Aside from where it pertained to armies and kings and governments, independence was overrated. For without God's help, where would she be? She depended on Him for everything. And perhaps a little too much on Buck Reiter.

At the base of the ridge, she stopped at a path little more than a deer trail cutting through the cottonwoods. A strip of flattened grass on either side bore witness to Buck's many wagon trips to the cabin. She tightened her grip on the reins and turned north. Her wagon was not as large and sturdy as his, but she trusted him not to set her on an impossible journey. Lifting her scrutiny from the road to the horizon, her pulse quickened at the silhouette of a lone horseman against the brightening sky.

Chapter 10

The Powell place lay southwest of the ridge, and Buck watched Lucy drive from the yard and along the meadow's edge. At the juncture, she hesitated then slapped the horse on. Her hearty "yah" carried up through the trees and spread a warm spot in his chest.

A month ago, he was set to take his string of mares and move on. Then he ran into Lucy Powell and her children at the mercantile and delayed his leaving. A week later, he thought to give her a few more days, help her get on her feet, then set out. The week after that, he shaved off his beard and reckoned one more week would do. And last week he held her in his arms and gave up on leaving her at all.

The creak of her wagon sounded beyond an aspen

cluster, and he nudged Charlie from the brush and onto the trail. Lucy drove round the trees and pulled up in front of him, her bonnet hiding her face and her young'uns grinning like opossums.

"Right on time." He leaned on his saddle horn and winked at Elmore. Lucy wore a fancy dress, not the same one she'd worn for so long. "You ladies look mighty fine this morning." Cecilia beamed, and Elmore pointed at his britches.

"You, too, Button." He reined Charlie around. "Follow me."

That morning before Buck left the ranch, he'd helped Nate carry the kitchen table out to the yard, and as they approached, a checkered cloth waved from it like a red-and-white flag. He tied Charlie at the house rail and helped the children from the wagon. When he reached for Lucy, she placed both hands on his shoulders and he swung her down. His heart raced ahead and he pulled his hat off and rolled the brim, waiting for words to catch up. She smelled fresh as the meadow after a rainstorm, and he swallowed hard. "You look...*mighty* fine, Lucy."

Her cheeks pinked to the color of her dress. "I thought you might be tired of seeing us in our everyday work clothes."

"I never tire of seeing you." The words were closer than he thought and fell out of his mouth without his say-so. A full flush rose on her face, and she turned to the wagon and reached for the bean pot beneath the seat.

"You made it!" His sister strode across the porch, down the steps, and around to Lucy with a hearty hug. "I'm Lilly and I'm so glad you came."

Lucy clutched the beans and flicked her eyes over Lilly's trousers. "It's nice to meet you, Lilly." She looked around with concern. "The children—they were right here."

Lilly waved off the worry. "Button and Sissy introduced themselves quite properly and they're in the kitchen helping Ara get things together. Darlings, they are. What a delight to have them here. It's been too long since I had a little one around."

Button and Sissy? Buck tucked away his pride as his sister took the beans and a basket over her arm and charged up the porch steps. "Come inside and we'll put these in the oven to keep. My, but they smell good. Buck said you make the best beans."

Lucy retrieved a Mason jar from beneath the seat but couldn't leave because he blocked her way. He longed to pull her close and ask her right then and there to marry him, but wouldn't that set the bees to buzzing. "I'll unhitch the mare."

She smiled, nervous, and nothing like the fiery, shotgun-wielding woman he'd startled a month ago. He touched her shoulder. Ran his hand down her arm and wrapped her fingers in his own. "I'm glad you came."

Lucy's arm still burned from Buck's touch, but she hugged her middle and bit her cheek while he regaled the children with the story of his nephew's courtship. Cecilia and Elmore laughed outright at Buck's tale, but they were children. Lucy merely *felt* like a child.

Everyone lounged back from the large table covered with the remains of cakes and pies and beans and beef. Lucy had eaten so much she felt as stuffed as poor Ara looked. Never had Lucy seen such a large and handsome young man as Nate Horne blush in utter silence, and never such a becoming bride as Ara, who was not only in the family way, but could be carrying the entire family all at once for the size of her.

"You really hid in the buckboard?" Cecilia turned wide, innocent eyes on Ara. "But Mama says—"

A quick swat to her leg and Cecilia's mouth clapped shut like a cellar door.

"What does your mama say, dear?" Ara rested her arms across her swollen belly.

"Her mama says she must mind her manners." Lucy's recent conversation with Cecilia burned about her neck and ears, but she smiled to assure Ara that all was well. And indeed, it felt so. The Hornes had welcomed her and the children like family, raved over her wild-berry lemonade, and cleaned up every last bean in her kettle. And Buck showed a playful side she'd not seen before.

Not that he'd had opportunity to play or relax when he

was busy stacking wood, building fences, or doing the other hundred things he did to help her. Here, in the comfort of his family, if he wasn't teasing his nephew, he was touching the children. A pat here, a hug there. And Button and Sissy, it was as if they were his own.

The thought snagged in Lucy's throat, and she covered her mouth with her napkin. Buck's hand found her back, gentle and warm.

"Are you all right?" His deep whisper fired chills up her arms and stole her breath, and she feigned a coughing fit. He refilled her glass with lemonade then handed it to her with concern tugging his brow.

With little more than a squeak, Lucy thanked him and envisioned Mr. Wellington trying to comfort his wife. Stifling a moan, she choked even further, bringing Buck's hand down firmly. She coughed in earnest, the wind nearly knocked from her. Holding up a hand, she shook her head. "I am fine. Truly."

His eyes darkened as he smoothed circles on her back and lit rings of fire inside her. "That you are."

If she didn't put distance between herself and this man, she was liable to beg him to marry her and show Cecilia what it meant to be two-faced and brazen all at the same time. "Let me help you clear the table, Lilly."

Ara also stood, and Buck's sister fired a warning look. "Sit."

As obedient as a pup, the girl fell back to her chair

with a chuckle. "Yes, ma'am!" But the way she rubbed her rounded self—even in front of the men—told Lucy the expectant mother needed rest. The baby might be early. Or the *babies*.

"Button." Buck jerked a thumb over his shoulder. "Got something in the barn for you." Elmore jogged away beside Buck's long strides as they made for the stables.

"And I have something for you." Lilly motioned for Lucy to follow her inside. The sprawling log house enclosed her in a welcoming embrace, and at once Lucy felt at home. But when Lilly handed her a pair of folded denim pants, Lucy stared.

"Buck said the two of you are riding out tomorrow to drive the herd down. These will make the chore a lot easier on you." Lucy blushed beneath the woman's bold appraisal. "They'll be loose on your slight frame, but they'll do. I'll find a belt for you, and one of my old shirts."

Lucy took the denims and shook them out. A puff of laughter bounced out when she held them against her. She looked up at Buck's sister, as tall and generous as he. "I will be the talk of the mountain in these."

Lilly laughed and hugged her around the shoulders. "You won't be the first, dear. You won't be the first."

That night Buck retired to the barn with Rascal, leaving his room for Lucy and the children. Delighted with such a large bed, Elmore crawled in first, a hand-carved willow soldier from Buck clutched in his fist. Cecilia snuggled in next, and Lucy followed. The children's excitement helped ease her discomfort at sleeping in Buck's bed.

Surprised that anticipation hadn't kept her up most of the night, she awoke the next morning to the children giggling and dressing before they dashed outside. Nervous beyond anything she'd ever felt, Lucy pulled on the denims and shirt, belting them as tightly as she could. She found Lilly in the kitchen pouring coffee into two china teacups. Apparently sensing Lucy's need to discuss weighty matters, the woman volunteered her story.

Lucy was right: Buck had made all the difference.

Chapter 11

Every muscle in Lucy's body ached as if she'd run down the mountain herself and not trailed the herd on horseback. But the animals seemed to know their way home, and she and Buck had merely encouraged them on through the woods and scrub brush and into the valley. Oh, that her pathway were as easily found.

Buck had ridden back to the Hornes's and brought Cecilia and Elmore home in the wagon with his horse tethered behind. He promised to return soon, in a day or so, after he found the fallen tree they'd come across. It'd make good firewood, he said. Lucy's heart lurched at his intentions, but she bit her tongue.

The children fell quickly to sleep that evening, their cheeks ablaze with sun and happiness, and Lucy welcomed her own exhaustion, praying it would silence her churning thoughts. Easing the front door open, she slipped out to breathe in the night. The corral creaked with an unfamiliar cadence as the cattle shifted and settled against the boards. Stars spilled across the moonless sky, and Lucy pressed a hand against her heart, imagining Buck atop the ridge. He was a good man. He would be a good father and husband. But she could not bear to be anything to him other than the woman he loved. She saw it in his eyes, felt it in his touch, but he made no mention of affection. What if her longing led her to believe what was not true? "Oh Lord," she whispered, "show me Your path."

The next day she fretted over Buck's insistence to drag out the fallen tree, and countless times she searched the pasture's edge for a rider breaking clear of the forest. When he did not return by sunset, fear snaked in and coiled around her insides. She couldn't breathe. Was he hurt as William had been? Trapped, unable to ride? Or had he simply decided not to return? To leave in search of new country and a mountain of his own.

Weary in heart and body, she tugged off her stockings that evening and combed out her braid. She hauled the rocker out to the porch. Huddling in a quilt, she strained to hear an approaching horse, a rider's hail, the scrape of a long pine dragging through the dark, colorless grass. Rascal curled at her feet with a puppy groan as if he carried the weight of her worries on his thin shoulders. What a ludicrous thought. As ludicrous as hoarding her troubles when the Lord waited to lift them from her. "I am no wiser than this poor dog, Lord." Her whispered prayer winged across the night and lit among the quaking aspen. She pulled the quilt tighter. *Bring him back to me, Lord.*

The meadow curled beneath its starry blanket, and still she remained, as fixed in her place as a cedar on the ridge. Crickets and coyotes lifted their voices, and she sank into the quilt, succumbing to the mountain song.

Waking at Rascal's yap, Lucy pushed against the stiffness in her limbs. The pup stood alert, nose pointing toward the wooded slopes, a whimper beneath its ribs in the pearly predawn. She bent to stroke the soft coat then scanned the dim meadow, dull and gray. There—at the tree line, something small and brown broke through, a rider cutting into the grass. Tossing aside the quilt, she bounded off the porch before the cry escaped her throat.

Buck scrubbed his face and looked again. Were the shadows playing tricks on him, or was Lucy running across the pasture?

His heart slammed into his chest. It *was* Lucy. He jerked the reins and hit the ground before Charlie stopped. Was something wrong at the cabin? Was Sissy hurt? Button?

At fifty yards he slowed and drank in the site of her— skirts hiked above her bare legs, her loose hair a dark and flying mane. And then she was in his arms, gripping him so tight around the neck he felt her hammering heart. The scent of her overcame him, the feel of her warmth against him, her breath on his neck. Her heartbeat slowed and her arms loosened their hold. As he set her feet on the ground, her hands slid around to frame his face.

"I—I was afraid"—she struggled for breath—"afraid you wouldn't come back."

He clutched her to him again and buried his face and hands in her unbound hair. "It took longer than I thought, but I'll always come back to you, Lucy. I love you more than life. You and those babies of yours."

She pulled back and swept his face with a yearning that burned clean through him. "Then marry us." The words struck lightning in her eyes and she clapped her hands over her mouth, a look of horror swimming above them.

Joy sprang deep in his gut, and he hauled her up and swung her around, his laughter drowning out the meadowlarks. "Marry you? You'd have this old cowboy with nothing to offer but a string of near-wild horses? No land, no money?" The sun broke over the ridge and lit a halo around her, and he set her down and pulled her hands from her lips.

"I'm so embarrassed," she whispered. Her eyes glistened, and her chin trembled as much as his heart.

Lifting both of her hands to his lips, he kissed her fingers. "You've read my soul, Lucy darlin'. Are you truly willing to be my wife and share a home and life with me?"

She smiled, and the dawn dimmed at her beauty. He dipped his head to catch her lips, and the taste of her was like honey in the comb, sweet and soft and full of God's promise he thought he'd missed. He scooped her up and carried her to his horse, set her in the saddle, and turned for the little cabin he called home.

Epilogue

Ara Horne's babies came early—halfway through August—a boy and a girl as fair-haired as their handsome father and dashing uncle who stood straight as pines at the head of the church.

Lucy had only one regret: that it was too late in the year for a columbine bouquet. But her wedding dress bore the color of her dear love's eyes, thanks to the insistence of Rosemary Wellington and Lilly's skills as a seamstress.

"It itches." Elmore ran his finger inside the collar of his new blue shirt.

"Shush, now. You don't want to upset Mama on her wedding day, do you?" Cecilia flounced her matching skirt.

Lucy bent to plant a kiss on each dear head then took their hands to await the pastor's signal. She had asked for a private ceremony, with only Buck's family, but she couldn't refuse the school board members, or her students' parents, or the Wellingtons who must have spread the word through town. Slowly, one smile at a time, people trickled into the sanctuary until the pews and Lucy's heart were overflowing.

At last the pastor joined Buck and Nate, and his brief nod told Lucy it was time. The path that lay before her and the children led to the man who had won their hearts and hers.

"Thank You, Lord," she whispered as she took her first step. "Thank You for helping me trust You to show me the pathway of life."

Davalynn Spencer is the wife and mother of professional rodeo bullfighters. She writes Western romance and inspirational nonfiction and teaches writing at Pueblo Community College. She and her handsome cowboy have three children, four grandchildren, and live on Colorado's Front Range with a Queensland heeler named Blue. Find her at www.davalynnspencer.com.

Also available from Barbour Publishing

Prairie
Summer
BRIDES

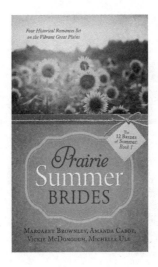

Four couples find enduring
love on the prairie.